All the King's Horses

Dandi Daley Mackall

SAINT LOUIS

Horsefeathers

Interest level: ages 12–16

Text Copyright © 2000 Dandi Daley Mackall
Published by Concordia Publishing House
3558 S. Jefferson Avenue, St. Louis, MO 63118-3968
Manufactured in the United States of America

Library of Congress Cataloging-in-Publication Data

Mackall, Dandi Daley.
  All the king's horses / Dandi Daley Mackall.
     p. cm. — (Horsefeathers)
  Summary: One month before sophomore year begins, Scoop volunteers to work with some newly donated horses at the Horsefeathers Stable.
    ISBN 0-570-07129-1
  [1. Horses—Fiction. 2. Orphans—Fiction. 3. Brothers and sisters—Fiction. 4. Aunts—Fiction. 5. Christian life—Fiction.]
I. Title.
PZ7.M1905 Al   2001
[Fic]—dc21   00-011893

1 2 3 4 5 6 7 8 9 10   09 08 07 06 05 04 03 02 01 00

In one month I'll be sitting in Ms. Dove's sophomore English class, staring at a blank sheet of paper, admitting that—to answer her question on what I did for summer vacation—I haven't done a thing. Nothing that counts."

Orphan sneezed and lifted her head. She nuzzled me before going back to grazing what was left of the south pasture grass. My horse is the best listener in the world. I scratched her neck under her long mane. Her black coat had a reddish tinge of sunburn. When I leaned into her shoulder, heat rose to my cheek.

I let out a sigh that made Orphan twitch at the withers. Maybe I was just bored. Maggie had been so caught up in summer stock theater that I hardly ever saw her. Carla had barely spoken to me since she'd gotten back from her vacation in Spain. *They'd* have plenty to fill up their English essay.

That morning, it had been boredom that made me step on the scales and straighten my back to the wall where we'd pencil-marked my height since I was waist-high. "Still 5′5″ and still exactly 110 pounds!" Dotty had announced, like it was something to celebrate.

Even my hair hadn't changed since the end of my freshman year, although the brown braid now reached my waist. I'd gone straight to the phone and called Carla to meet me at Horsefeathers for a ride. Carla hadn't said much, but she did grunt an *uh-huh,* which I took as a yes. Only I'd been waiting over an hour and she hadn't shown.

Orphan's muscles tensed. She jerked up her head and craned her neck around. A horn honked across the pasture, from the lane. I recognized the *barru-u-ga* of Dotty's old Chevy and the screech of her brakes.

I jogged to meet my aunt as she pulled up to the barn. Swiping at the sweat dripping from my forehead, I came around to the driver's window. "What's up, Dotty?"

My aunt still had on her orange apron uniform Mr. Ford makes the check-out employees wear at the Hy-Klas Grocery Store. Her short brown hair stuck to her forehead in sweaty clumps, and her glasses sat crooked on her broad nose. She tried to rest one chubby arm out the window, but the metal door must have burned, and she tucked her arm back inside.

"Hey, Scoop!" Dotty always sounds so glad to see me. Anybody eavesdropping would have thought we hadn't seen each other in months, instead of hours.

"Why aren't you at work?" I asked, shooing a fly off my shoulder. I'd kind of lost track of time, but Dotty rarely got home before sundown, and the sun wasn't down.

"Mr. Ford let me off early. We ain't had enough customers today to fill a thimble. I reckon folks is staying home out of the heat." Dotty patted the seat next to her, where she'd tried to cover a tear in the upholstery with a giant X out of gray duct tape. Dust puffed up with tiny pieces of white stuffing. "Come on with me to pick up B.C."

It took me a second to remember where my brother was. "B.C.'s at King's Kamp, right?" I don't know how I could have forgotten. Dotty had forced him to go to our church's summer day camp three days already, and you'd have thought she was sending him to a firing squad with a bulls eye painted on his chest.

Picking up my brother was bound to be better than prying him out of the car to drop him off. Still, I didn't feel like doing anything. "I don't think so, Dotty."

"I betcha you'll change your mind when I tell you what I heard tell down at the Hy-Klas." Eyebrows raised, eyes wide, she waited for me to beg her to go on. When I didn't, she burst out, "King's Kamp is getting theirselves some horses!"

"Horses? You sure, Dotty? Where did King's Kamp get horses? What are they planning to do with them?" I was already moving around to the other side of the car and reaching for the passenger door. The metal handle burned my fingers as I grabbed it and slid inside.

"I ain't got the slightest notion, Scoop. Reckon we oughta go see for ourselves?" She turned the key in the ignition, even though the motor was already running. The car moaned in protest.

"Where's Carla?" Dotty asked as she circled in front of the barn and bounced back down the dirt path. "I thought her and you was going riding."

I shrugged. "Carla's probably with Ray." I glanced out the dirty back windshield at my stable and the crooked sign: HORSEFEATHERS STABLE—HOME OF THE BACKYARD HORSES. The near-drought had robbed Horsefeathers of color, leaving gray dirt in front of the barn to blur into the gray barn wood. The pond had been shrinking steadily.

"Better start praying for rain, Dotty," I said, sticking my hands between the seat and my bare legs. My cutoffs stuck to the plastic, and my white T-shirt was gray with sweat.

Dotty stopped humming. "A dry spell like this here one makes a body 'preciate God's rain like nothin' else, I reckon. Mr. Ford, he says today, 'Dotty,' he says, 'if we could make rain and sell it at the Hy-Klas, we'd be millionaires!' So I says to him and Lou—Lou, he stops chopping up beef to hear—I says, 'And to think our heavenly Father gives rain for free!'"

I didn't feel like talking, so Dotty went back to humming while she drove to King's Kamp. The drive took three verses of "Amazing Grace" and four of "How Great Thou Art," holding the last "Art" of each verse way too long.

I'd never gone to camp, even though our church is one of the main sponsors of King's Kamp. Dotty and I weren't as into God when I was B.C.'s age. As we passed the baseball diamond and basketball court, I wondered why my brother hated it so much.

Two boys who might have been B.C.'s age, 11, sat on a bench, probably waiting to be picked up. Two more were tossing a football a few yards away, just out of the reach of twirling sprinklers. I didn't see B.C. ... or horses.

Dotty stopped in the middle of the road. She didn't seem to notice the two cars that screeched to a stop behind us. She got out and inhaled deeply. "Ain't this fine? King's Kamp even smells good!"

One of the boys hopped off the bench and ran to the end of the line of cars now stacked up behind us like a train wreck. I got out, avoiding eye contact with the drivers.

"You can't park here!" A woman with her arms full of folders stormed up to us. "No, no! You must move!" She was tall and broad-shouldered, with thick, sandy hair pulled back in a giant barrette. If she'd been a horse, she might have been a Jutland, the favorite horse of Viking invaders.

"Howdy do!" Dotty exclaimed, putting out her hand to shake, as if they were old school buddies.

The Jutland woman had her hands full and couldn't shake hands with my aunt. But she didn't look like she would have anyway. "You are blocking traffic."

"Dotty Eberhart," said my aunt, her hand changing directions to push up her glasses. "This here is Scoop. Say, you people run a mighty fine camp out here!"

The tall woman shifted her weight from one leg to the other, the way a horse will before he steps on you. "Parents are waiting to pick up their children."

"So is aunts." Dotty giggled.

The woman's face grew splotchy red the nicer Dotty got. I figured I better do something before she had a heart attack.

"We're here to pick up B.C.," I said.

"Ah," she said, nodding once, as if that piece of information explained everything. "The Cooper boy. I was wondering when we were going to meet Ben's parents."

"It's *Coop*," I said, knowing I should explain about how we hadn't had parents for nine years. But my stomach knotted. People always get this look when I say my parents are dead. Then they ask how, and I have to explain about the explosion, and the deeper they ask, the deeper it digs until I hurt all over again.

Dotty came to my rescue. "Scoop and B.C. and me, we live together since their folks moved on to heaven."

The Jutland woman frowned as if she wasn't sure what that meant. She still hadn't given us her name. "Let me see if I can find your ... Ben," she said, moving off toward a big, brick building.

A couple of cars behind us were turning around by driving over the curb and jerking backward and forward. Dotty waved to them.

"I don't see any sign of horses, Dotty," I said, letting my gaze sweep the premises. In the middle of one field was an old barn. Three men stood on the roof. "Is that Pastor Dan?" I asked, squinting into the sun. Our pastor is so skinny he's easy to pick out, even from a rooftop.

"Hey there! Pastor Dan!" Dotty waved so hard the flab on her arm jiggled.

Pastor Dan waved back. I didn't have to be there to know not a speck of flab jiggled on *his* arm. Dotty would have liked nothing better than to fatten him up. He's the same age my dad would have been.

He scurried down the ladder and ran across the field to meet us. "Dotty! Scoop!" His plaid shirt was soaked through with perspiration. He used the shirttail to swipe at the rivers of sweat trickling down his balding head. "Have you come to join King's Kamp, Dotty?" His smile took up his whole face.

"Ain't right sure how's Mr. Ford would take to that," Dotty said.

"How about you, Scoop?" he asked, turning to me.

I shrugged and studied my dusty tennis shoes. At the beginning of summer, Pastor Dan had asked some of us kids to help out at camp, but I'd said no. Travis was the only one who'd volunteered.

"What do you think of our barn?" he asked, friendly enough. "We could use an expert's opinion, Scoop."

"You're really getting horses then?" I asked.

"That would depend on who you ask." He rotated his head and cracked his neck. "If you ask me, *yes*. God has seen fit to come up with some healthy, homeless horses, and I think King's Kamp is the perfect place for them." He glanced behind us and lowered his voice. "Not everybody agrees with me."

The Jutland woman was doing the Tennessee running walk toward us. "Hasn't Ben shown up yet?" she asked. She'd left her folders someplace, but still held a very sharp pencil.

"Dotty, Scoop, this is King's Kamp's newest social worker, Ms. Mansfield," Pastor Dan said. "Have you met Dotty Eberhart and her niece, Sarah Coop? Call her 'Scoop.' And her brother goes by 'B.C.'"

"Have you seen him, Pastor?" she asked, without answering his question about ever meeting us.

"I think I saw B.C. and David running toward the bathrooms, but that was quite a while ago," he said.

Ms. Mansfield, who was a head taller than Pastor Dan, had shifted her attention to the road. She squinted over his head at a cloud of dust that billowed from the camp entrance. The line of cars behind ours had pulled out one by one, and I could make out what looked like a trailer approaching.

"What on earth—?" asked Ms. Mansfield, frown lines swallowing up her whole face.

"Look at that!" said Pastor Dan, with a wink to Dotty and me. "That must be the horses God's delivering to our doorstep."

"That can't be!" exclaimed Ms. Mansfield. "We are not ready for live animals on the premises."

I wondered if that meant she wouldn't have

a problem with *dead* animals on the premises, but I kept my mouth shut.

The trailer pulled up behind Dotty, and I recognized it before it came to a stop. "Horsefeathers! Dalton Stables?" I asked, as stunned as if the trailer had been driven by Elijah. Daltons operate the richest stable in our part of the country, but nobody has ever accused them of being generous. "*They're* giving away horses?"

Pastor Dan grinned. He knew the Daltons as well as I did, even though technically Ralph Dalton is my uncle. I'm the branch of the family tree he'd just as soon prune.

"Ralph bought out a stable in Kidder, lock, stock, and barrel," Pastor Dan explained. "I understand he sold several of the horses and had a handful he has no use for."

"Let me guess," I said, things coming into focus. "*Those* are his gifts?"

"Doc Snyder checked them all out. She says they're sound as a dollar, Scoop."

Stephen Dalton and his dad climbed down from the trailer. They both looked air-conditioned cool, their dress shirts dry and wrinkle-free. "What are you doing here, Scoop?" Stephen asked, his beady, scum-colored eyes narrowing to slits. His face looked sunburned, and so did his hair, which shined redder than blood.

"Nice to see you too, Stephen," I said.

Ralph Dalton said polite hellos to everyone.

"I'm in rather a hurry. Just tell us where we can unload the—"

"Absolutely not!" Ms. Mansfield's voice was so loud everyone else stopped talking. One of the horses in the trailer stamped his hoof.

"I don't understand," Ralph Dalton said, narrowing pea-green eyes that looked a lot like Stephen's.

"King's Kamp is simply not prepared to take on horses. You'll have to take them back." Ms. Mansfield glared at Pastor Dan.

"I know we don't have things ready yet, Ms. Mansfield," said our pastor. "And I admit the horses will need a little work."

"We don't have staff to train horses," she insisted. "Take them back."

"We can't do that," Ralph Dalton declared. "We closed the Kidder stable. And these horses don't belong at Dalton Stables, even if we did have room for them, which we don't."

"Be that as it may," said the unmoved Ms. Mansfield, "they cannot stay here."

Pastor Dan turned and pleaded with her. "It could be such a wonderful experience for the boys, Mona."

Ms. Mansfield shook her head. "I'm sorry. I really am. It just can't be done. We're under-staffed as it is."

Dotty's lips moved, and I knew she was talking to God.

"Very well," said Ralph Dalton. "I just wish someone would have informed us before we drove all the way out here."

"Wait!" I cried.

Stephen and his dad stopped, each with his hand on a door handle.

"Take the horses to Horsefeathers," I said, before I really knew what I was saying. "We'll work them until they're safe for King's Kamp boys." The pieces were clicking together. This was the thing I was meant to do for my summer vacation. I could single-handedly save these horses.

Ms. Mansfield's frown deepened. "I still don't know if—"

"Please!" I tried to think of what Maggie would have said to convince this woman. "You can count on me, Ms. Mansfield. King's Kamp has done so much for my little brother." Dotty cleared her throat, but I kept on. "B.C. adores this place, and I'd like to pay back King's Kamp for what it's done for him."

The moment was interrupted by a scream of terror, a scream I recognized with horror as coming from my little brother. All heads turned as B.C came racing out of the restroom building like he was on fire. He didn't stop yelling until he parted us like Moses at the Red Sea and fell down on his knees in front of Dotty.

"I hate King's Kamp! I hate it! I hate it! Get me out of here! They're trying to kill me!"

2

I forced a nervous laugh as my brother glued himself to Dotty's ankles. "B.C., you're such a kidder."

"What say you and me go wait in the car?" Dotty asked him. She hobbled to the car with B.C. still attached to her legs.

"Scoop makes a good offer, Mona," Pastor Dan said, sounding like he was on my side. "We have enough in contributions to pay for the horses' boarding fees at Horsefeathers for a month."

"But our boys don't even know how to ride," said Ms. Mansfield, staring after my aunt and brother.

"I'll teach the boys to ride," I said. "*We'll* teach them, at Horsefeathers. They can come to our stable for lessons a couple of times a week while the horses are there. And we'll work with the horses in between times."

I could sense her weakening. "No one would be allowed to so much as touch a horse until I personally met with the parents," she said.

"I need to do something with these horses," said Ralph Dalton.

"I just don't know—" Ms. Mansfield glanced at the trailer, then at Dotty's car. "I guess it won't hurt to take the horses to Horsefeathers for the time being."

"Thank you!" I cried. "You won't be sorry."

"I am not committing the camp to anything until I talk with each and every parent!" Ms. Mansfield shouted after me as I ran to the car.

I hopped in before she could change her mind. "Go, Dotty!" I said, snapping my seat belt. The car felt like a sauna. I'd never been in a sauna, but the intense dry heat felt just like Carla had described it after her vacation to Sweden.

"Drive fast, Dotty!" I urged as we pulled away from King's Kamp and the Dalton trailer. "I want to get things ready at Horsefeathers before the Daltons get there."

"Drive faster!" B.C. echoed from the back seat. "Get as far away from this place as you can. I hate it there! I'm not going back, and you can't make me!" His green shorts and black T-shirt bunched on him in a million wrinkles, and his hair stood up in greasy spikes.

"What did you do to your hair, B.C.?" I asked, twisting around to see him better. He looked like he'd been ridden hard and put away wet.

"*I* didn't do it! *David* did it! He gave me a swirly!"

"A *swirly?*" Dotty asked, still driving at the speed of dark—slower than a tractor.

"That's what David calls it when he holds me by my ankles and dunks me in the toilet and flushes it. He hates my guts!"

Dotty turned to look at B.C. The car wandered off the road, and she pulled it back. "Is that where you was, B.C., honey? You was in the bathroom getting yourself flushed? We'd best invite that boy and his kin over for supper and have us a little talk about—"

"No, Dotty! Don't! Promise! Don't tell David where I live! I told him I live in Canada!" His voice grew louder, and he slapped the car seat over and over.

"Okay, B.C.," I said. "We won't invite him." I didn't have to ask my brother why the kid picked on him. B.C. would be the smallest fifth grader in his school come fall. "What's this kid's name?"

"David," B.C. muttered, like he was spitting out a mouthful of sour oats.

"David what?" Dotty asked, still driving so slowly the Dalton trailer was gaining on us.

"Just *David,*" B.C. said.

By the time we got to Horsefeathers, the Dalton trailer was right behind us. I hopped out. "Thanks, Dotty. I might be late getting home."

"Don't you need B.C. and me to give you a hand with all them horses? We'd be glad to help, wouldn't we, B.C.?" Dotty said, her hand headed for the ignition key.

"No, that's okay," I said. "Really. Thanks. I just need to get the horses settled." The last thing I wanted was to worry about B.C. leaving a gate open or Dotty getting stepped on. "You better hurry off before they block the lane."

"Well," she said, fingering the gray-tape X on the empty seat, "if you're sure. But me and B.C. don't mind—"

"I'm sure." I motioned for Ralph Dalton to pull up. Jogging over to the trailer, I caught sight of Orphan, her neck stuck over the paddock fence. She whinnied impatiently.

Dotty edged the old Chevy past the trailer. "Bye bye!" she shouted, waving out the window.

"I hope you know what you're doing," Stephen said as he climbed down from the trailer. I was pretty sure he was hoping I *didn't* have any idea what I was doing.

One peek in the trailer told me we were taking on four horses. With our six, that made 10 boarders. "No problem," I said, mentally assigning stalls and horses and pastures.

Stephen's dad didn't look happy. His hairspray had melted, leaving his too-black, too-thin hair to fend for itself. He was an irritable Barb, the quick-tempered breed ridden by Bedouin tribes. "Would somebody tell me where to put these horses?" he asked.

I wanted to unload them myself, in my own time, getting to know each horse individually before introducing them to the Horsefeathers horses. But I knew he'd never stand for that. "In—in the paddock?" I said, hating how weak my voice sounded.

"I guess we can stay and help you get them settled," said Ralph Dalton, consulting his watch.

"That's okay," I said too quickly. I wanted them to leave even more than they wanted to go. I moved to the back of the trailer and let down the tailgate ramp.

The closest horse, a Palomino I sized up at 14.2 hands high, nickered as I untied her lead rope. She was a nice-looking gold, the color of an ice cream cone, with short, white socks on her hind legs and a lean Quarter Horse build.

"What's her name?" I asked Stephen, as I led her easily down the ramp and turned her in the dusty drive.

"How should I know?" Stephen griped. "Who cares anyway? They're not registered."

Stephen always gives my horse a hard time just because she's not registered. But Orphan is worth more than the whole of Dalton Stables, if you ask me.

"I think they called her Babe," said Stephen's dad, waving his arms to shoo a horsefly.

I handed Babe's lead rope to Stephen and

went back in for the next horse, a Blue Roan big enough to have been a draft horse. "You're a big fella," I said, patting his broad rump. Dust clouds billowed from his mottled coat, making me cough. "And a *dusty* fella too."

The gelding's coat was black-brown with so many white hairs that it looked bluish. I suspected some of the white hairs were from aging. He sighed and turned half-closed eyes to me when I untied him. I started toward the ramp, but he didn't budge. "Come on ..."

I hollered down to Stephen, "What's this big gelding's name?"

After a minute, Stephen's dad called in to me, "No idea. Do you need help getting him out?" His tone was edgy.

"Nope!" I shouted. I tried pulling the Roan to the left, then to the right. He didn't even lift a hoof. He wasn't fighting me or resisting. It was more like he didn't know what I wanted him to do. "Come on ... Dusty," I coaxed.

Then for no reason, he decided to follow me. His giant hooves clamored down the ramp, rattling the tailgate with every deliberate step.

"This is the one that took us an hour to walk from the stable," Stephen said, reluctantly accepting the rope I handed him. He'd passed Babe off to his dad. "Good luck with this dumbox."

I stroked Dusty's thick neck under his matted, gray mane. Then I headed back inside for

Horse Number 3.

"Be careful of the Pinto," warned Ralph Dalton. "His name is Bruiser. I'm assuming there's a reason they called him that. Leave him last. The Chestnut shouldn't give you any problems, unless he's scared to come out. I think they called that one 'Red.'"

As soon as I'd worked my way back to the horse, I could see why they'd called him "Red." He was a Red Chestnut, with a lighter, flaxen mane and tail. If he'd carried himself better, he could have been handsome. But cowered in the corner of the trailer, he looked pathetic.

Nothing about the horse spelled danger, so that was good anyway. There's a spooky kind of scared that makes a horse a walking time bomb. Red didn't have that wide-eyed look of an accident waiting to happen. When I stepped toward him, he trembled but showed no signs of defending himself. His ears rotated, trying to take in every sound.

"Scoop?" Ralph Dalton shouted in through the air vents. "It's getting late."

Trying to hurry so the Daltons could go home, I reached too fast for Red's halter. He jerked his head back and slammed into the wall. "Easy, Red," I told him, keeping my arms down at my sides. "Nobody's going to hurt you."

Red didn't want to come out of the trailer with me, but I made him, pulling firmly until he gave in. It's not what I like doing, and it's not the way I work at Horsefeathers. But Father and Son Dalton were putting on pressure, asking me every two seconds if I needed help.

Stephen had tied up Dusty, the big Roan, to the nearest tree, which never would have held that horse if he'd decided to bolt. But Dusty swished his tail and stood motionless, grateful for the shade.

I handed Red over to Stephen. "Don't do anything to frighten him," I said.

"Whatever," he said, sighing like his father, a silent scream to hurry up.

The trailer was turning into an oven. The last horse was another gelding, a stock-type Pinto, powerfully built through the hocks and withers. When I tried to scratch his withers, something most horses love, he pulled away. I stroked his neck, but he tossed his head. He didn't seem to like being touched. But he came out of the trailer like a good-natured Morgan.

"You're no Bruiser, are you, boy?" I murmured as he followed me over to the tree where Dusty was tied. "We can turn them out in the paddock," I shouted to the Daltons as I took Dusty's lead. "Follow me through the barn."

We paraded through Horsefeathers' barn. Dusty tried to munch from every hay bale we passed. Bruiser kept as much distance between himself and Dusty and me as the rope allowed.

"This red horse is a wimp!" Stephen said, chuckling behind me. "He's scared of his own shadow." He turned the Chestnut loose, and Red trotted to a empty corner, bolting away from Orphan and the colt Misty, who came to welcome him. None of the new horses herded into a group or even paired up. It was hard to believe they'd lived together.

"Are you sure you'll be all right here, Sarah?" Ralph Dalton asked, letting Babe go. The Palomino didn't hurry off, but the Daltons did.

"I got it under control," I said, turning my two charges loose in the paddock. Dusty didn't budge, but Bruiser seized the opportunity to declare himself boss. He charged poor Red, wheeled around, and kicked. His hind hooves missed Red by a couple of feet, but Red squealed as if he'd been attacked.

Apparently, Dusty thought kicking was what we wanted of horses, so he sent up a thick-hooved buck that barely left the ground. The Palomino tossed her head and reared in short, nervous leaps.

"You got it under control all right," Stephen called, scurrying out of the paddock. He plopped over the fence, then shouted, "Somebody's coming!"

Great. All I need is more people.

Through the dust came Travis Zucker's

white pickup. Maggie and Jen were in the cab with him. Travis is a senior, two years older than we are, and probably the best looking guy in the world. His hair is as gold as Babe's Palomino coat. If Stephen Dalton were a pesky Shetland, Travis Zucker would be a noble Palomino or maybe a Salerno, the handsome Italian warm-blood—strong, capable, and easy on the eyes.

Orphan and Misty were the only two Horse-feathers horses in the paddock with the new stock. Their friendly attempts to meet the new horses got rebuked at every turn. Instead, any movement by Orphan or the colt stirred up the others, fueling their frenzy, sending them bolting and racing around the paddock, bumping into each other, then tearing off in the opposite direction.

"Scoop! Have y'all gone and lost your li'l ol' senses? Wherever did you get these darlin' creatures?" Maggie 37 Brown was having one of her Southern Belle days, pouring on the Southern accent to perfect it for her theater career.

I gave up trying to settle the new horses and made my way to the fence.

"I, for one, like what you've done to the place," Travis said, his white teeth shining from his deeply tanned face.

Travis' sister Jen, our treasurer, raised her eyebrows at me. "Care to explain?" she asked.

"Aren't they wonderful!" I exclaimed,

although the dust they were kicking up kept us from seeing too clearly.

"My goodness," Maggie declared. "I am in love with that big Roan! Just look at his adorable whiskers!"

"My father donated these horses to King's Kamp," Stephen explained.

"You're kidding. Right?" Maggie said, giggling.

"Tax write-off," Jen said, without taking her eyes off the paddock.

"They're a little rough around the edges," I admitted. "I volunteered to work with them so they'd be okay for King's Kamp boys."

"Scoop," Jen scolded, "we cannot afford—"

"They can pay us for a month," I explained quickly. "And that's perfect for us, right? We have a month before school starts to fine-tune the horses. Then they'll go to King's Kamp."

"Do they even have kids at that camp who can ride?" Jen Zucker can ferret out problems quicker than a horse finds honey.

"I kind of volunteered to teach the King's Kamp boys to ride ... here ... on these horses."

"I can't believe Ms. Mansfield would go for this," Travis said. "Have you met her? This sure doesn't sound like the Ms. Mansfield I know."

"It isn't," I said. "I mean, it's all my idea. I told them we could get the horses ready and then teach the boys—"

"Scoop!" Jen scolded, as if she were years older, instead of weeks. "Look at these horses! What if we can't get them ready for the kids?" She wheeled around to the Daltons for the answer.

"Don't look at us," Stephen said.

Ralph Dalton frowned. "If we can't donate the horses, we'll have to take them to Kennsington."

"Kennsington?" I asked, wondering why he hadn't taken the horses there in the first place. "You know someone in Kennsington who wants these horses?"

Jen looked serious, but she didn't say anything. Ralph Dalton stared at his shoes. Stephen covered his mouth, as if he were holding in a laugh.

"What?" I asked, feeling the tension build.

Travis put his hand on my shoulder. "Scoop," he said gently. "Kennsington has a slaughterhouse."

3

After we got rid of the Daltons, Travis and Maggie climbed into the paddock with me. "Good thing we came early, huh?" Maggie said.

Early? I'd forgotten all about our scheduled Horsefeathers meeting. Was I ever going to get some time alone with the horses? Besides, it had been Jen's doubts and problem-hunting that forced Ralph Dalton into saying what he did about the fate of the horses if we couldn't get them in shape.

"Do you ... " I almost couldn't get the words out. "Do you think he meant it, Travis? Would Ralph Dalton really take these horses to the slaughterhouse?" I shivered, even though it felt like 140 degrees in the paddock.

"Yeah, he'd do it," Travis said. "One of the guys I worked on the road with said he sold his gelding for slaughter last winter and got $700 for him." Off and on during the summer, Travis had hired on with a construction crew, digging and lifting, repairing potholes between West Salem and Kennsington. He said the money was great. But Maggie and I decided the tan and muscles he'd come away with would have been pay enough.

I watched Bruiser, the Pinto, pace back and forth along the fence. The other horses had settled down. Orphan stood between Babe and Red, no doubt filling them in on the secrets of Horsefeathers. *I am going to keep these horses out of the slaughterhouse,* I promised myself, *if I have to work every minute of every day.*

Travis helped me turn the new horses out of the paddock and into the south pasture. I was pretty sure Carla's horse Ham, Buckingham's British Pride, wouldn't get along well with Bruiser or Dusty. Even Cheyenne, Jen's horse, might pick a fight and get in over her head.

I closed the gate between the pastures, just in case, leaving Orphan to look out for the newcomers. Misty put up such a fuss, I had to let him in with Orphan. The colt would be safe with Orphan looking after him.

Babe, Red, and Dusty took a few steps, then set about the serious task of grazing the short, fading grass poking through dried, cracked earth. Not Bruiser. He paraded around the pasture like he owned the place and dared anyone to say he didn't.

We gathered into the little Horsefeathers office, where a tiny metal fan stirred up hot air. Travis stayed to give us a better idea of what

King's Kamp was about. Maggie and I scooted up on the desk, and Jen took the desk chair, leaving the folding chair for Travis.

I was about to call the meeting to order when I heard footsteps in the stallway.

"Good!" Maggie said. "Carla's here."

Ray and Carla strolled in together, hand-holding up to the second they stepped inside. Ray and I have been friends longer than Carla and I have. Ray was there the day my parents adopted me and brought me to live in West Salem. And he was there the day they died in an explosion at the bottle plant, where they both worked. Ray and I had never been anything except friends, but it still felt weird seeing him with Carla.

I waited for Carla to give me some excuse why she'd stood up Orphan and me on the morning ride. But she acted like nothing was wrong.

"Hey," Ray said, plopping on the hay bale and tugging Carla down beside him. "If Travis can stay, I can stay." He stretched out his long legs. Even I had to admit they made a good couple. Carla, with her shiny black hair, perfect body and complexion, was one of the prettiest girls— if not *the* prettiest in high school. Lanky Ray would have been a Tennessee Walking Horse if he'd been a horse—easy-going, but with his own confident style.

"Your hair looks great, Carla!" Maggie said, hopping off the desk to get a closer look. "Did you get it cut in Spain?" she asked, reaching for Carla's hair. Carla jerked and looked to Ray.

Ray let out a nervous laugh I don't think I'd ever heard from him. There's nothing fake or nervous about the guy. "In Spain? Her haircut?"

Carla seemed to paste on her smile. "I'm sorry, Maggie. Yes. In Barcelona. Thank you." Carla is hearing and speech impaired, so it sounded more like: *I soy, Mayee. Yeah. 'N Bar-uh-lone.* With her new style, multi-layered, shoulder-length hair covered both of her hearing aids.

Maggie slipped back to the desk. Carla stared out of the office, while Ray changed the subject. "So what's up with the new horses out in the pasture?"

As quickly as I could, I filled everybody in on the horses and King's Kamp, and what I'd volunteered to do.

"I think it's terrific!" exclaimed Maggie 37 Brown. Maggie's real middle name is "37," given to her at birth, on March 7 (3-7) by her mother, who says her lucky number was already 37. But Maggie, in search of the perfect stage name, changes her last name as often as she changes her clothes—and usually to the same color as her clothes. Tonight, since she had on green shorts and a green tank top, she was probably calling herself "Maggie 37 Green."

"Here's what I think we should do," Maggie said. "Each of us—*real* members, that is—should take one horse and train it. Then we can divide the King's Kamp kids ..."

I sat back and listened as Maggie launched into a whole plan. Even though I was officially in charge of the meetings, it happened like this every single time. Maggie always took over. Words spilled out of her like grains of oats. My words just sat there, like giant blocks of salt.

"And before we go any farther," Maggie said, as if anybody was going anywhere except her, "I put dibs on Dusty, the giant Blue Roan out there. He looks like a big, cuddly bear. I am going to devote the whole, entire day tomorrow to training Dusty."

Travis raised his hand, then grinned and lowered it. "If I'm permitted to speak, I think Jen should take the Palomino. What's her name?"

"Babe," I said, glancing over to see how Jen would take her brother's interference. Jen Zucker has a serious kidney disease. Lately she'd been doing great with new medication. But that didn't stop her big brother from looking out for her.

"Let me guess," Jen said. "Babe is already well trained?"

I shrugged. "None of the horses are wild or spooky. I think they're all safe. They just need a good riding." I didn't appreciate everybody getting in on the act. I had a gut feeling that if I could handle each horse myself, they'd all be ready inside a week. But I wasn't the one in charge.

"Yikes!" Maggie said, after grabbing Travis's wrist to check his watch. "I have a date. Let's see. Carla, which horse do you want?"

Carla hadn't been paying attention. Ray had to elbow her. "You decide," she said. "We didn't get a good look at the horses. It's probably too dark to see much tonight."

"Okay," Maggie said, scooting off the desk and rearranging her dreadlocks. "Why don't you take the Pinto?"

"The Pinto is the only horse I'm not sure of," I said. "He's kind of a bully with the other horses, and they called him 'Bruiser.' His ground manners seem fine, and he probably won't be any problem. But I should probably take him myself, just to be on the safe side."

Carla stared at me the whole time I spoke. "And you don't think I could handle the Pinto?" she asked, her tone razor sharp.

"I didn't mean that," I muttered.

"Then I'll take Bruiser," she said. She stood up. "Night, everybody." She left, with Ray right behind her.

"Is something going on with you and Carla?" Jen asked after they'd gone.

"Not that I know of," I said.

"I'm off!" said Maggie 37, hurrying out of the office. "I'll come by in the morning and get started with Dusty. Bye!"

Travis and Jen exchanged grins. Then Travis counted, "1, 2, 3, 4, 5, 6, 7—"

Maggie came tearing back. "I forgot! Silly me. I came with you, didn't I!" Her whole body seemed wound, ready to spring.

"Something tells me Maggie is in a hurry," Jen said, scooting back her chair and closing her notebook. "I have plans in the morning, but I'll try to get out in the afternoon to get to know Babe."

We all knew when Jen said she "had plans," she had a doctor's appointment. "No rush," I said.

They moved out together. "Scoop," Travis said, "I'll take a trip out to King's Kamp and see what I can learn about our ... our future riding students."

"Good," I said. "Thanks."

When they drove away and the rattle of Travis's pickup faded, I gazed up at the stars popping out. No people noises invaded Horsefeathers, nothing but whinnies and nickers. This was how I liked Horsefeathers best—just me and my horses.

Orphan whinnied from the pasture. I met her at the fence with a handful of oats before heading home. "Take care of the new kids," I told her.

Dotty was folding church bulletins at the kitchen table when I walked in. Even though I couldn't remember the last good rain we'd gotten, our house still smelled musty. I hadn't noticed that the night had cooled off outside until I was greeted by the dead heat inside our living room. I tripped over B.C.'s shoe and kicked it out of my way.

"Scoop? That you?" Dotty called. "How'd them horses fit in at Horsefeathers?"

"Fine, Dotty," I said, crossing over to the sink and getting out a glass. The first two glasses I took down were dirty. I let the water run, hoping it would get colder. It didn't. Lukewarm water continued to sputter out, hitting the black chips in the white enamel sink and splattering up. I shut off the faucet and tried the fridge. "Can I have the juice?"

"We have juice?" B.C. asked. He was plinking bottle caps together at the table. Once a week Dotty folds bulletins, and B.C. counts them into stacks, then holds down the piles with his bottle caps—"bottle caps them," he calls it.

I downed the orange juice in two gulps. It was so sour I wondered how long it had hidden there in the back, behind pickles and olives. But it was cold.

"Can't they find anybody else to do that?" I

asked, seeing the unfolded mound of bulletins.

"Now why should they go and find some other bodies?" Dotty asked. "B.C. and me is doing just fine, ain't we, B.C.?"

" 'Sides," B.C. said, "who else has enough bottle caps to hold down the piles?"

"Ain't that the truth," Dotty said.

"I'm taking a bath and going to bed," I said. "I'm beat. And I have to start in early on the horses."

"They better be nice to Misty," B.C. warned. "Or I'll send them all back to King's Kamp. And *I'm* never going back there!"

"Well, we'll see about that," Dotty said. "Lord, help me and B.C. see our way clear to Your answer on this here problem. More bottle caps. Good night."

Dotty talks to God so natural, it's almost like it's not prayer. I'm sure she had already told Him all about B.C.'s problem. I'm sure He was already working on an answer. But B.C. understood the "more bottle caps" was directed to him, and he arranged his caps on a new stack of bulletins. I understood the "Good night" was for me, and I said good night.

That night I fell asleep while I was praying about the new horses. Sometime in the night I had a horrible nightmare. I saw a herd of horses—Babe, Red, Dusty, and Bruiser. But Orphan and Moby and Cheyenne were with them. Stephen Dalton was driving the horses with a huge whip, and I tried to get to him to make him stop. But Maggie, Jen, Carla, and Ray were blocking the way. They kept talking like I wasn't even there, like they didn't notice what Stephen was doing.

The horses kept getting farther and farther away. And then I saw where Stephen was taking them. The fog cleared, and a broken-down, red brick building lay ahead of the herd, directly in their path. I strained to read the sign posted on the front of the building. The letters slowly came into focus: *Slaughterhouse*. The horses were being driven to their death.

4

I thought I'd never get back to sleep after my nightmare. Finally I dozed off, but it was so late that I overslept. When I came downstairs, Dotty had already left for work, and the sun was well on its way to baking the house.

B.C. sat in Grandad's old rocker, rocking a hundred times faster than my grandfather had when he lived with us. The TV blared.

"Aren't you going to camp?" I shouted over squeaky cartoon voices.

B.C. kicked the rocking up a notch. He was holding an opened box of Tastee-O's, Dotty's favorite Hy-Klas cereal. Toasted little O's flew out like confetti. "I'm not ever going!" he screamed, not turning from the television. "I hate it! And I hate those kids, and they hate me." He seemed to be shouting at the animated robot man on the screen. "And especially David hates me, and I won't go and you can't make me, and Dotty said I didn't have to because, well, I forget because why, but I won't go."

I'd kind of hoped B.C. could be my spy at

the camp and find out how the other boys felt about horses. But he sounded so close to manic, I knew not to bring up King's Kamp again. Most of the time, my brother acts pretty normal. But his highs are higher, and his lows go lower than most people travel. Plus, B.C.'s emotions can switch leads faster than a cow pony around the rodeo barrels.

B.C. tipped the rocker back and jerked it just in time to keep from spilling out. Tastee-O's filled the air. I opened my mouth and caught a few of the Os as they shot past me—breakfast.

Before I left, I filled two plastic water bottles Dotty had brought home from work. *Hy-Klas has klas!* was written on the sides in flaking orange letters.

"See you, B.C.," I said, as I eased out the screen door.

The sun filled the pale blue sky the way a bright light fills a small room when you first turn it on. The ditches and bushes crackled with grasshoppers. If we didn't get rain before long, we'd be buying hay at high prices all winter. One good rain could still bring up enough grass to give us a fall mowing.

As soon as I turned up Horsefeathers Lane, I heard Orphan nicker from the pasture. She couldn't get into the paddock to meet me at the fence as usual, so I ran to her. Not only the colt, but Red and Babe followed Orphan up to the pasture fence.

"You didn't waste time making friends, did you, Girl?" Suddenly all I wanted to do was ride, to feel Orphan beneath me and forget about everything else. I climbed the fence and slipped onto Orphan's bare back. Leaning forward, I let her know, without words, what I wanted.

She responded with a playful buck that sent her into a gentle lope. Her warm, black neck arched as I hugged it, and I breathed in her fresh, earthy scent. I closed my eyes as she cantered to the end of the pasture. The only sound was horse music. It plays in my head in perfect moments when the wind rushes over Orphan and me. Prayer and praise that usually have to be pulled out of me, now came as easily and free-flowing as heaven's breeze.

"Walk," I whispered, and Orphan reluctantly obeyed, her hooves springing on the hard ground as she hoped I'd change my mind. "We can't let everybody else go hungry just because we're having too much fun."

The other horses had stayed at the fence, close to the barn. I suspected Misty had told them that's where breakfast would be served. Even Dusty had the right idea. He pulled up a mouthful of grass and chomped on it as he strode lazily toward the barn.

Bruiser eyed us from a few yards away. His spotted coat looked as clean as when he'd arrived at Horsefeathers. The other horses looked dirty or dusty enough to assure me they'd either rolled in the pasture or at least taken a quick lie-down. The more relaxed and secure a horse feels, the freer he is to lie down. Only a contented horse will roll and leave himself vulnerable to attack. Apparently, Bruiser still didn't trust us.

I hopped off Orphan and raced to the barn, where I dumped oats as fast as I could. Outside, the old timers neighed in protest, and the new-comers nickered in anticipation.

1-2-3-4-5-6-7-8-9-10. I counted the stalls, double-checking each trough. When the horse version of musical chairs ended, I didn't want anybody left without breakfast. Dogless, our barn cat, trailed me from stall to stall, meowing for his morning meal.

"You'll just have to wait," I told him. *"The last shall be first."* It was something Dotty liked to quote. Dogless didn't appreciate it any more than B.C. and I did. He stood over his empty food dish and cried.

Making sure all the grained stalls were open and the other stalls closed, I left the barn and crossed the paddock. Ten horses scolded me for taking so long. "I know this doesn't look fair," I said, apologizing to the new horses as I unlatched the other gate first. *"Company first, right?"* That was another of Dotty's sayings. "But these guys already know which stalls to run to. Okay?"

I pulled back the pasture gate. Cheyenne crowded through first, followed by the other Horsefeathers' horses. They trotted or cantered into the barn, splitting off to their appointed stalls.

"*Now* it's your turn," I told our guests, unlatching their gate. Bruiser, who had been the last horse to come to the gate, now bullied his way to the head of the line, sending poor Red in retreat. I eased back the paddock gate and let the newcomers in.

Bruiser barged through and galloped past the barn before darting back. He wanted the first stall he came to, even though it was already occupied by Cheyenne, the one horse who wouldn't mind fighting him for it. Cheyenne squealed when Bruiser tried to nudge her out. She kicked, missing the Pinto and sending him to hunt for a different breakfast. He didn't like it, but he settled for the stall next door.

The Palomino Babe was next through the gate. She was fine until she heard Cheyenne and saw Bruiser bolt from the stall. Then she froze, her four legs braced, her shoulder twitching nervously.

"That's okay, Babe," I said. She let me scratch her withers until she relaxed. Finally, she let me lead her into an empty stall next to Orphan.

By the time I came out of the barn again,

good ol' Dusty had plodded across the paddock and was headed, sensibly, for the nearest empty stall and full trough. That left Red. The Chestnut still hung back in the pasture, not venturing past the gate. From the looks of him, he needed the grain more than any of them. Two ribs rippled his reddish coat at his chest.

"Come on, Red," I said, reaching slowly for his halter. He squealed and jerked his head up, then stared at me pitifully and wide-eyed. When I slid my hand to his halter and tugged gently, he didn't move. When *he* got scared, he just balked—irritating, but not dangerous to ride.

Finally, Red gave up and followed me into the barn. But by the time we got there, the other horses had finished their grain. Bruiser had downed his own breakfast and gone looking for more. He'd found the uneaten oats and was greedily finishing them off.

I led Red to a different stall, closed the back door, and gave him his own breakfast to eat in peace.

"Yoo hoo! Anybody here but us horses?" Maggie 37 Black sauntered down the stallway, dressed in black tights, a black body suit, and a short, black wrap-around skirt.

"Morning, Maggie," I called from Red's stall.

She stopped outside the stall as I came out. Anyone who didn't know better would have assumed that she was dressed for one of her dance or aerobic classes. But I knew better. Maggie was going through a jazz phase with her voice teacher. She felt dressing in black helped her get in tune with true jazz, whatever that means.

"Voice lessons?" I asked.

"How'd you guess?" she asked. "Has Dusty finished eating? I only have an hour to work with him."

I should have known better than to believe Maggie could devote the whole day to Horse-feathers, even if she had believed it herself the night before. "You don't exactly look dressed for riding," I said.

"I'm not going to ride, silly," she said.

"You're not?"

"Not today. I don't have time. But I *am* going to work with Dusty. I'll start him on the lunge line." Maggie turned on her heels and strode to the tack box before I could tell her Dusty didn't need the lunge line.

"I'll cross-tie him for you so you can groom him," I said, moving down to Dusty's stall.

"That's okay," Maggie said, meeting me with the lunge line. "I don't have that much time. I'll just lunge him now. Then I have a trick I can't wait to teach him."

Maggie's horse Moby knows more tricks than any horse I've run across. She can count, nod, rear, lie down, roll over, pull scarves out of pockets and hats off heads. But I had a feeling Dusty wasn't going to be such a quick learner.

"You better at least brush him, Maggie," I called after her.

Dusty let me lead him out to the cross-ties. I had to stand on tiptoes to snap the ties to his halter. He let out a deep sigh as Maggie brushed his wavy mane.

By default, I had been left with the Red Chestnut. Maggie had seen to that when she doled out Bruiser to Carla. As I groomed Red in his stall, he relaxed and let himself enjoy it. "It would sure help if I knew the history of this horse," I said loud enough for Maggie to hear from the cross-ties.

"How come?" she hollered back.

"I think Red was abused, maybe a long time ago. But he hasn't forgotten it. That's why he's so scared of everything." Red didn't like having me shout. His ears flicked up and back, rotating to pick up signs of danger.

"Well, Dusty," Maggie said, "come on." I heard her grunt. "What's with you? I don't have all day!" More grunting and coaxing came from the stallway.

After a few minutes, Maggie cried, "Scoop! Why won't this big lug move? I'm running out of time!"

I returned Red's brush to the tack box and joined Maggie and Dusty. He'd only moved a couple of feet from the cross-ties. Maggie was using the long, green nylon lunge line as her lead rope. "I don't think Dusty knows what a lunge line is," I said, unsnapping it and handing it back to Maggie.

"So what?" She took it and glared at Dusty *and* me.

"Hand me the lead rope so he's sure what you want," I said.

Maggie rolled her eyes, then tossed me a plain lead rope. "How could he not know what I want?"

I shrugged and snapped on the rope. "Ready?" I asked him. Turning my back to the Roan, I stepped forward. I took up slack in the rope until I felt Dusty give in behind me. He followed me at his own pace out to the paddock, where I handed him over to Maggie.

"Thanks," she muttered. "*Now* we're going to put you on the lunge line, Dusty." She said each word distinctly, as if talking to somebody hard of hearing. "Get it? This little ol' line goes like this. You stand there until I get in the middle of the paddock." Maggie walked to the center of the paddock arena as she talked. "Now, you walk in a circle around me."

Dusty stayed where he was.

"Walk on!" Maggie commanded.

Dusty lowered his head to search for a nonexistent blade of grass.

I couldn't watch any more. I went back for the second lunge line, then headed to the south pasture with Red. Red had obviously been lunged before and was anxious to please. Walking, trotting, and cantering on voice cues, he moved in a wide circle around me.

Maggie 37 didn't fare as well with Dusty. From time to time I heard her shout out Dusty's name in at least four different accents. I hoped she'd have a voice left for voice lessons.

About a half hour later, Maggie walked out to meet me in the pasture. "I give up," she said, looping the long lunge line around her hand and elbow, lariat style. "Either Dusty is having a bad day or that Blue Roan is the dumbest horse I've ever met."

"Maggie!" I scolded. "Dusty's not dumb." I brought Red in, anxious to get him out for a ride.

"Not dumb? That's what *you* think," Maggie said, brushing hairs off her tights. "I couldn't even teach him to nod yes. How am I going to teach that old horse new tricks?"

Before I could object, she added, "I know. Moby's probably older than Dusty. So it's not just old age. Something tells me that giant horse has a tiny pony brain."

"Dusty's not stupid, Maggie," I insisted, taking the wound lunge line from her. "He's just not on your time schedule."

"Ooh! Speaking of time schedules, I have to run! Ms. Tibbits hates it when I'm late. See you!" She took a short cut through the pasture and out to the lane.

Maggie 37 is probably my best friend. It's just that sometimes, just like with Dusty, Maggie and I aren't on the same schedule.

I cleaned and adjusted a bitless hackamore for Red. I had just swung up on him bareback when I spotted Travis's pickup coming up the lane. Red's back was sharp and bony, not comfy like Orphan's. I gave him the slightest pressure of my knees, and he responded, breaking into a trot. In 30 seconds, I knew the horse neckreined and responded to voice commands. He'd be a good horse to give lessons on.

I urged Red to the fence and waved at Travis as he got out of his truck. Instead of the usual, amazing Travis smile, he looked so serious I felt my chest tighten. "Travis, what is it?" I shouted. "Is it Jen? Is she okay?"

He shook his head and made a feeble attempt at a reassuring grin as he met me at the fence. "Jen's fine, Scoop."

Relieved, I sat up straight and pivoted Red left, then right, just by laying the reins on his neck. "You had me worried," I admitted. "So what is it? Did you just talk to Maggie? Don't believe a word she says about Dusty. He'll come around. They all will. I'm just getting started."

"Why bother?" he asked, slumping over the top fence rail.

"What are you talking about? These horses will be good lesson horses for the King's Kamp kids."

Travis squinted up at me. Something was going on, and I didn't like it. Travis Zucker is one of the least pessimistic people I've ever met.

Red must have sensed I was getting anxious. He began sidestepping nervously. I slid off of him. "Out with it, Travis."

"I don't know, Scoop," he said. "What good will it do to train the King's Kamp horses if you don't have any students? Nobody at King's Kamp wants to ride."

5

"Horsefeathers, Travis!" I cried. "*Nobody* wanted to ride the horses?" Never in my wildest dreams had I considered that one. I'd imagined every other kind of problem. But the possibility that healthy, all-American boys wouldn't *want* to ride? No way.

"I tried my best, Scoop. I was at King's Kamp this morning before it opened. Ms. Mansfield had already called the parents for a special meeting. Eight of the boys had at least one parent there with them."

"And?" I urged.

"And she gave them her version of what taking riding lessons at Horsefeathers would be like," Travis said, raking his fingers through his thick, blond hair.

"What do you mean *her* version?" I asked. Red nudged me from behind. I ignored him.

Travis shook his head. "Scoop, you should have heard her. By the time Ms. Mansfield finished talking about liabilities and 'equine risk' and accident statistics, I don't think *I* would have signed my life away—which is what she said they'd need to do before their boys could set foot here. She had a stack of papers for each guardian—"

"It's not fair! I wish I'd been there myself!" I cried.

"I did try, Scoop," Travis said.

"And nobody saw through her? Not even one kid wanted to ride anyway?"

"Actually, one kid *did* want to ride," Travis admitted.

"Who?"

"I don't know," Travis said, rubbing his forehead. "Miller, I think. Something Miller."

"Well," I replied, "that's a start."

"His parents weren't crazy about the idea, to put it mildly." Travis let out a dry chuckle, as if he'd just remembered something. "And there was one father who wanted his son to take horse riding lessons. But you should have heard the kid. As soon as his dad said anything about riding, the little boy burst into tears. Eric. That was his name. Eric Rudd. I remember because his face got red when he cried. And he has red hair."

"So that makes two!" I insisted. "That's not *nobody!* Travis, we could get that one kid ... Eric ... to love horses. I know we could. And his dad's already in favor of it, right? Call him and tell him we can handle his son! Promise him we'll help Eric get over his fear of riding."

Travis stopped leaning over the fence and started looking more like the real Travis, but with more muscles and a deeper tan from his work with the road crew.

"What about the other kid?" I asked. "Something Miller?"

Travis shook his head slowly. "That Miller kid was a real brat, Scoop. He kept screaming at his parents, saying that he *knew* how to ride and they had to let him do it. It wasn't pretty."

"Great! If he's a brat, then he's probably still screaming. Call his parents too, Travis. That boy has probably worn his parents down by now, if he's anything like B.C."

"Or Tommy," Travis said, grinning.

Travis's brother Tommy isn't such a bad kid. If he lived in the city, instead of on a farm with eight brothers and sisters, he'd probably be known as "street smart." If he'd been a horse, he would have been a feisty Shetland. Even though Tommy and B.C. would both be going into fifth grade, they lived in different worlds. In fourth grade, Tommy made a small fortune selling his sister's old homework papers—until Jen got on to him.

I could almost see the wheels turning in Travis's head. "All right, Scoop. Say that you're right and I can persuade the Millers and Rudds to sign up for King's Kamp riding lessons at Horsefeathers. That's still only two students. Ms.

Mansfield made it perfectly clear she'd scrap the whole project if we didn't have at least four students: *'Four horses. Four students.'*" Travis' attempt at mimicking Ms. Mansfield wasn't mean-spirited, but it made me laugh.

"Well, we've got the four horses," I said, thinking out loud. "If you get Miller and Rudd, I can get B.C. to sign up."

"I thought he quit King's Kamp."

"He did," I admitted. "But I'll sign him up again. I think I can sell him on the lessons. He wouldn't even have to go back to the camp. What about Tommy? I'll bet he'd love to take riding lessons."

"I'm sure he would, but he's never gone to King's Kamp."

"Not yet," I said, grinning.

"Scoop," Travis said, eyeing me as if he couldn't quite recognize me, "this is a whole new side of you. Don't get me wrong—I've always known you could get *horses* to do whatever you wanted them to. But people? You don't suppose you're becoming a *people*-gentler too? Scoop, the *people whisperer?*"

I felt my face heat up in a major blush, which should have answered Travis's question about me and people.

"Hey! I almost forgot!" Travis nodded toward his truck. "Come see what I've got."

Red had been standing so patiently behind

me. Since I refuse to tie a horse with his bridle, even for a few minutes, I slipped the bridle off and let Red go free. Travis waited for me while I climbed over the fence. I felt his hands clasp around my waist and lift me the rest of the way down. When he let me go, I could still feel him. I was afraid to speak. I knew my voice would quiver.

"I almost forgot about these," he said, striding over to the truck as if his fingerprints weren't still on my waist. "To be honest, I didn't think we'd have any use for them."

He let down his tailgate and showed me. "Ta-dum!" Travis's truck bed was loaded with saddles.

"Horsefeathers, Travis! Where did you get them?" I fingered the closest saddle, a mid-sized Western model badly in need of saddle soap. The leather was cracked, and the lining cushion all but bald.

"More tax write-offs for the Daltons. I know—they're old," he said, pulling the other saddles close enough to scrutinize. "I had to drive out to that stable they closed down. These four were what the King's Kamp horses were using."

I could already tell that those four were the only saddles worth keeping. The others looked like they'd been run over by a horse trailer. We carried out the good saddles and set them on saw horses in the tack room. "Let's see what we've got," I said, wiping off each seat with a barn rag. "All this crud should come off with saddle soap and neat's-foot or linseed oil."

Two of the saddles were identical, dark leather with narrow saddle horns. Nothing fancy, no carvings or doo-dads, but the construction was okay. "It's great they're all Western," I said. "It would be harder to try to teach Western and English at the same time."

"Let's see if I can remember which saddle went with which horse," Travis said, using his T-shirt to shine the silver studs on the only show saddle. It was black, silver-studded all over the fork, the skirt, the back of the cantle, and around both fenders. Larger silver spangles decorated the big hood covers on both silver-plated, wooden stirrups. All that metal and leather weighed down the saddle, making it twice as heavy as the others. But it must have been a showy piece of tack once upon a time.

"The guy at the stable said the fanciest saddle went with the fanciest horse, the Pinto. What's his name?"

"Bruiser. He's the bully of the lot," I said. "Maybe he demanded the best saddle."

"This one ..." Travis patted a plain, well-worn saddle that was oversized, with long flank billets and latigo, front and rear saddle straps. "This one went with—"

"Let me guess," I said, stretching out the long girth meant to go around the horse's belly. "Dusty, the big Blue Roan?" The saddle, with lengthened straps and cinch, was rigged for a work horse. It was probably the only saddle ready to ride.

I examined the two matching saddles. "These will work for Red and Babe, but we'll need new straps, front and rear, and new girths." It would be fun going to the saddle shop with Travis.

"Jen and I can pick them up in Hamilton," Travis said.

I'm pretty good at hiding my disappointment. "Will Jen have enough time, with training ... and everything?"

"Sure," he said, heading back outside. "Jen's got the Horsefeather's checkbook, right?"

"Yep. This should just about drain the account. But we'll be okay again when we get the King's Kamp boarding fees."

"I'll go call the Millers and Rudds right now. And I'll see about signing up Tommy." Travis climbed in his truck and turned the key. The engine coughed twice before it turned over. "Get B.C. on board. When do you think the horses could be ready?"

"I don't think the horses need much," I said, leaning in so I could hear him over the engine rumble. It was Friday, and I counted days in my head. "If I can work these horses through next week, we can start a week from Monday." *If I don't run into trouble with Bruiser.* I felt pretty confident about the others.

"That fast?" Travis asked. "That would be great—the last two weeks of camp." He shifted gears. The truck groaned. Then he turned his famous Travis grin on me. "Don't forget Who's really in charge, Scoop."

Who's really in charge? Maggie? Is that what Travis thinks? Or Jen? She's in charge of the checking account, but that doesn't mean she should run the riding camp.

Travis glanced up at the sky. At heaven. I felt like an idiot. He meant *God* was in charge. At least I hadn't let on what was going through my head.

As Travis's truck disappeared in clouds of dust, I tried to pray. *Sorry I haven't been working things out with You in all this. I get so wrapped up making things work, I just forget. Will You help me remember to pray more? Give me horse memory.* God made horses with memories that would shame an elephant.

My stomach was growling, but I couldn't break for lunch until I'd had at least one ride on Bruiser. I was hoping they called him Bruiser because he acted the bully with the other horses. *That,* I could handle. In any group of horses, one will rise to the top as the resident boss.

What worried me more, as I took a lead rope out to the pasture, was that Bruiser didn't like to be touched. Usually, horses that don't like to be touched have lost trust in humans. But I didn't think that was the problem with Bruiser.

As I approached the Pinto, his pupils followed me, but he didn't look fearful. He kept grazing up to the minute I snapped on the lead. Then he let me lead him easily. But when I stopped to stroke his withers, to search for his favorite grooming spot, he sidestepped away. No matter what his problem was, it would be pretty hard to bond with a horse who wouldn't let me touch him.

Bruiser followed me quietly through the paddock as my mind raced over possible strategies for training each of the horses. I considered teaching methods we could use once we got our students. Bruiser was right behind me as I stepped inside the barn and let my eyes get used to the relative darkness.

"What do you think you're doing?" Carla Buckingham stepped out of the shadows, dressed in English gear from her bowler to her breeches.

"Carla! You scared the life out of me." She's only two inches taller than me, but she seemed a foot taller in her riding boots. I stared at the tiny, white Polo pony on the front of her pink knit shirt. "I didn't know you were coming today."

"Apparently not," she said, her big, brown

eyes narrowed to slits. "You know very well that *I'm* in charge of Bruiser." Her voice got louder, and her speech more tangled and hard to understand. *"In—foot-er, I woo uh-pish-ate it if you—"*

"Slow down," I pleaded. "I can't understand you."

Carla's face hardened, and I saw her clench her fists. "Give—me—that—horse," she said clearly, separating each word from the one next to it. "And then just get out of my way!"

6

I stared stupidly at Carla as she jerked Bruiser's lead rope out of my hand. "Carla, what did you just say?" I asked. Carla wasn't what you'd call a regular church-goer, but I'd never heard her be so rude before.

"My speech still is not clear enough for you, Scoop?" she asked, sparks in every word. "Tell me this then. Why did you feel you had to start in on the Pinto? Why didn't you start with Jen's horse, or Maggie's, or—wait, here's an idea—*yours?*"

"But I—I mean, you—the Pinto—" I couldn't explain, not with Carla glaring down her perfect nose at me. I would never figure out Carla Buckingham, no matter how long I lived.

Carla had moved to West Salem and into the biggest house in the county the end of our eighth-grade year. We hadn't exactly gotten along from Day One, but we'd been through a lot since then. We'd become friends. Still, every time I thought I was getting to know her, every time I was stupid enough to believe she thought of me as a friend, something like this happened.

I took a deep breath and tried again. "Look, Carla. I was just going to give Bruiser a quick ride. I have to know how much work he's going to need before we can use him for King's Kamp lessons." It made me mad that I felt like I had to explain myself to her. Why was I making excuses for riding one of the horses at *my* stable?

"That's what I thought," she said coldly. "Thank you for bringing Bruiser in from the pasture. I'll take it from here." Carla turned and led Bruiser to the stallway.

"Carla!" I shouted after her. "I know you don't want help. But that horse doesn't like to be touched. I wasn't going to make him stand in the cross-ties. He'll feel better being groomed in a stall or outside." I said it loud enough that I knew she could hear me, even without her hearing aids.

Carla ignored me and walked straight to the cross-ties. She snapped in Bruiser and got brushes out of the tack box without so much as a glance in my direction. When Carla Buckingham, daughter of Edward Buckingham III, wanted to, she could make me feel like a big zero, like I was the hired hand and she was Lady of the Hunt.

"Fine," I muttered. But my mind didn't stop with *fine*. *Of course Carla Buckingham knows best. How stupid of me! Her father's a famous international lawyer. My father was a factory-worker, and he's dead. Same for my mother. But her mother is a ... another lawyer. My horse isn't even registered. Her horse is the Tri-State American Saddlebred champion, Buckingham's British Pride.*

Still dueling inside my head, I stormed back to the pasture and brought in the Palomino. Babe let me lead her in by the halter to the barn.

Carla had finished—or given up on—grooming Bruiser, who still stood in the cross-ties. I knew she was headed for the tack room. When she saw me across the barn, she stopped in the stallway and squinted at me.

I decided the best tactic would be to act like everything was okay and I wasn't mad. "Travis brought us a bunch of Western saddles," I shouted so she could hear me across the stallway. "So we're going to teach everybody on those. It should be easier to get them all going on Western tack. The black show saddle was Bruiser's."

Carla kept staring at me. "Oh. I see." She nodded, and I was pretty sure I saw a quick smile before she left for the tack room.

Good. I'd kept my head, and Carla had come around. If we couldn't be best buddies, at least we could work together.

Relieved, I led Babe out to the paddock, where I brushed her and cleaned out her hooves. None of the horses had shoes on, but they'd had their hooves trimmed recently. And that was how I liked it. As long as they weren't ridden on the roads, the horses would get along best unshod. Their hooves would harden and grow out healthier when they moved to the King's Kamp pastures.

I tried a couple of bridles on Babe before settling on a one-eared snaffle, an old reining bridle I had in the bottom of the tack box. I didn't see Carla again until I heard her lead Bruiser outside. I adjusted Babe's bit, then looked up to ask Carla to hold Babe while I went back for a saddle. "Carla, would you mind—"

I stopped. What was the matter with Carla Buckingham? After everything I'd said about giving the boys Western riding lessons, after I'd described the saddle I wanted her to use on Bruiser, she'd gone ahead and tacked him up English. There he stood, with Carla's English saddle, the irons dangling halfway down his side. His build was stocky, like a Quarter Horse, and he looked ridiculous in the tiny no-horn saddle.

Carla smiled at me. Then with perfect posture, perfect technique and style, she mounted. "We're off," she said. "Wish us luck."

Luck? What does she need with luck? She's got all the answers. I turned my back on Carla and eased Babe's reins over her head. It felt like Carla was mocking me, pretending to listen to my advice about saddles and then totally blowing me off. Worse than that, she was ridiculing me—doing the exact opposite of what I asked her to do, and then smiling about it.

Right again, Ms. Buckingham. Scoop always rides bareback. What would she know about saddles? I kept busy with Babe's forelock until I heard Carla ride off. Then, instead of going in for a Western saddle for Babe, I jumped on her bareback. If Carla could ride English, then I could ride bareback.

For the next hour, we rode our mounts in the same paddock arena, but we might as well have been on opposite ends of the world. We didn't exchange words, not even eye contact, as each of us put her horse through its paces.

Sneaking peeks when Carla rode in front of me, I was surprised to see how easily the Pinto handled. Bruiser tensed up for the trot. But who wouldn't, I reasoned, with Carla Buckingham on his back, posting up and down like a yo-yo?

Babe didn't need such a long workout in the sizzling heat, but I was determined to outlast Carla. Even though my stomach growled, making the only human noise in the arena, I held my ground until Carla quit. She left Horsefeathers without saying good-bye.

As soon as she was out of sight, I cooled down Babe and headed for home. It was mid-afternoon, the hottest time of the day. All I could think of was something cold to drink and the leftover roast chicken Dotty had brought back from the Hy-Klas the night before.

When I stepped onto our driveway, I heard the television blaring, something Western, with galloping and gunshots. B.C. had obviously been playing ball on the front porch. Every piece of sports equipment he'd ever owned lay strewn over the railing or scattered on the wooden steps. To get to the screen door, I had to step over a deflated basketball, a black bouncy rubber ball, and two smashed ping pong balls.

The door didn't fly open the way it usually does at the slightest nudge. I had to shoulder it. As I shoved my way inside, a pile of books toppled over. An empty box lay tipped on its side. Dotty's favorite lamp, the porcelain dog lamp with a yellowed shade, slid backward on the floor. It was still on, still plugged in, but sitting in front of the door.

Sliding in carefully, watching every step so I didn't crush anything, I set the lamp back on the phone table and pulled the gold chain on the dog's nose to turn it off. The room was still plenty bright, lit by sun streaks speckled with dancing dust. Sunlight poured through smudged windows, making them look dirtier than ever.

The living room looked like a herd of wild horses had run through it. The rocking chair lay face down, tipped over in the dirt-tracked shag carpet, as if bowed in prayer. Newspapers and magazines covered the couch. The floor was a minefield of tiny, plastic toys.

"B.C.?" I asked, fear closing my throat and making my voice crack. Every sign was pointing to another burst of my brother's manic depression, the hyper, wild side of his disease. Dotty calls it *his disease*.

"B.C.!" I shouted, my heart pounding. When he's depressed, I think that's the worst time, the awful silence or the crying jags. Then he gets hyper, and I think *that's* the worst time. It's the scariest time. The anything-can-happen time.

In the kitchen, dishes littered the counter, some from our regular mess, but most of it new. The chicken I'd been thinking about all afternoon was spread out on the kitchen table. He'd taken one bite out of each piece.

I ran to B.C.'s little bedroom. Twice I tripped over plastic horses, *my* plastic horses. He must have gotten them off my dresser and brought them downstairs. Why? But there was never a *why* when B.C. got like this. Or if there was a *why*, it wasn't the question that screamed in my head. There was only a *what*, followed by a *how bad?* or *how far?*

B.C.'s bed was stripped clean, but it was the only clean thing is his room. I'd been waiting for the bottle caps. The more manic B.C. gets, the more meaning his bottle caps take on for him.

When our dad used to come home from his shift at the bottle plant every night, he'd bring B.C. a pocketful of bottle caps. I can still remember the clinking sound of metal on metal as Dad stuck his hand in his pocket. "Bottle caps?" he'd ask, as if he'd never heard of such a thing. B.C. couldn't even talk yet, and he'd sit in front of the screen and reach up tiny hands. Then when Dad pulled out the caps and dumped them at B.C.'s bare feet, my brother acted like he'd been given diamonds and candy bars. That's how we started calling him B.C.—B.C. for "Bottle Cap."

A metal clinking jarred me back to the present. I froze, confused. I was hearing the music of the bottle caps. I turned toward the screen door, as if I expected Dad to walk in again, his pockets weighed down by nine years of bottle caps.

I heard the clanking of metal again. But it was coming from the bathroom. "B.C.?" I yelled, stumbling toward the bathroom. He didn't answer. I pressed my ear to the door and heard bottle caps clanking and water running.

"I'm coming in, B.C.!" I screamed. I turned the knob and threw open the door.

B.C. had his bottle caps stacked along the bathtub. Water filled the tub and trickled out over lone caps and onto the floor, where more bottle caps held their ground like river boulders. Water overflowed the sink, where B.C. had built a tower of bottle caps two feet high. He didn't seem to know I was in the room.

"B.C.," I said calmly, "I'm shutting the water off now." I slipped behind him and turned off the tub faucet. Then I reached in front of him and shut off the sink faucet. My arm brushed his bottle cap tower. The tower swayed. In slow motion, it crumbled. The caps flew at us, bouncing off skin and falling on the floor. It sounded like the drum section of a kindergarten band.

"Now look what you did!" B.C. cried. "Look what you did! You broke it! You ruined everything!" He swung at a smaller tower on the edge of the sink and knocked it over. I dodged the flying bottle caps and prayed neither of us would get hurt.

B.C. tore out of the bathroom. I stumbled after him. He headed for the front door, stomping everything in his path. As he passed the television, he stopped. His head jerked sideways, and his gaze locked on the screen.

Without making a sound, I sneaked in behind him and righted the rocking chair, scooting it up to his legs. Still staring intently at the TV, B.C. reached back for the arm of the chair. He eased into the rocker and gripped the sides like he hoped it would fly off with him.

The bald man on the screen stared back at my brother, telling him how hard it was to get a date once you lose your hair, how all you notice is how thick other men's hair is. B.C. hung on every word, as if this TV man had the answers to life's greatest problems.

If B.C. would stay there, rocking and watching, I wouldn't have to call Dotty home from the Hy-Klas again. Dotty's boss, Mr. Ford, understands about B.C., but he has a store to run.

Quietly, I stepped back to the bathroom,

trying not to set off the toy minefield hidden in the carpet. I drained the tub and the sink, checking on B.C. every two seconds. It took all the towels we own to sop up the water on the bathroom floor. People in our county were on a water alert not to water their lawns until the level at the reservoir came back up. I wondered if we'd get in trouble with the law for watering our bathroom.

B.C. rocked his way through the infomercial about miracle hair-growing stuff. He rocked softer through a black-and-white rerun of "I Love Lucy," never breaking into so much as a grin. Meanwhile, I picked through the debris in the living room, rescuing my four plastic horses and pitching everything else into the cardboard box.

Curious what else B.C. might have taken from my bedroom, I carried the horses up the stairs, their stiff, plastic bodies clicking against each other as I hugged them to my chest. I have the attic room. It's the coldest room in our house in winter, the hottest in summer. Even with the window wide open, heat gathered in the top of the A-shaped ceiling and slid down, spreading out waves of sunless heat.

As I turned into my room, I braced myself for whatever B.C. might have done to it. One glance told me nothing had been taken but the statue horses. I lined them back up on my dresser, the black one first, the bay next, followed by the white and the Paint.

The only other thing out of order was that my jars had been moved. Over a dozen clear, seemingly empty jars sat in a jagged circle on my unmade bed. The jars weren't empty though. They're part of my collection of air, a tradition I'm carrying on from my grandad.

When Grandad died, he left a basement full of jars, all of them filled with air that marked days worth remembering. Instead of keeping pictures in scrapbooks or writings in journals, Grandad captured the air of moments and things he didn't want to forget. He'd lived long enough to have jars labeled with events from WWII and the Kennedy assassination, my dad's birth and my dad's death.

I'd only been collecting air since the day of Grandad's funeral. It surprised me to see how many jars I had already. I knelt beside my bed to grab an armful of the different-shaped jars and return them to my dresser. No two jars were the same. They ranged from jelly and pickle jars to Mason jars, one caviar jar, and a fancy cut-glass container Mrs. Powers gave me.

I picked up the tallest, skinniest jar. It had held black olives until they went bad in our refrigerator. Now the jar was full of air from a fresh, spring day when Orphan and I cantered through tall, green grass that swayed in our breeze as we passed. I'd spotted a doe and her baby lying in a clearing. Orphan and I had watched as the mother studied us and decided she didn't have to worry.

As I stared at the air from that perfect moment, I wanted to smell the wild bittersweet, the sharp tinge of hedgeapple, and the sweet clover again. I wanted to open the tiny white lid and feel the air brush against my cheek, the same air the doe had breathed. But I didn't. I set it back, along with the other jars, and hurried downstairs to check on B.C.

Halfway down the stairs, I sensed the change. Just like that, fast as the switch of a horse's tail, B.C.'s mood had shifted. He still sat in the creaky rocking chair, but it had stopped rocking. The creaking hadn't registered in my brain until now, when the chair kept silent.

B.C. wore the same dazed, television stare, but his toes didn't tap. His fingers didn't cling, and his hands rested in his lap. He hadn't changed channels, even though his station barely came in anymore. Static that sounded like paper rustling drowned out the TV voices.

I shut off the television, and he didn't react. "B.C.," I said, squatting in front of the rocker. "You okay?" I'd seen B.C. depressed so often, I knew the answer to my question. He was not okay. There were only the other questions: *How bad? How long? How deep?*

B.C. slumped back in the rocker and pulled his knees up to his chin. I'd have to call Dotty.

Putting off the call as long as possible, I walked to the kitchen and threw out the chicken. It already smelled dead. I pulled a half-eaten can of pork-'n'-beans from the fridge and ate it in the archway, where I could keep an eye on my brother.

I was out of good daylight hours to work the horses, but I'd still have to go back to Horsefeathers and feed them. Joining B.C. again and kneeling by his rocker, I looked hard into his eyes, trying to see what could possibly be behind those eyes, in his brain, causing so much pain, a pain that was way too big for him to handle. "B.C., I have to go to Horsefeathers and do chores. Do you want to come with me?"

No answer.

"Will you be okay if I go fast and come back fast?"

He didn't blink.

I went to the phone and dialed the Hy-Klas. The phone rang five times before somebody picked up.

In between gum-smacking sounds, a girl's voice said, "Yeah? Hy-Klas."

The young voice threw me, but I thought I recognized it. "Gail? Is that you?" Gail Gayle, Mr. Ford's niece-in-law, had worked for a few weeks at the grocery store when I was a freshman. Actually, Dotty had done most of her work for her. I could picture Gail, tall, thin, dressed in black, sporting more pierced earrings than her ears could hold.

"Yeah, it's Gail," she answered, not sounding very happy about it. "Who's this?"

"This is Scoop, Dotty's aunt. I mean, Dotty's *my* aunt." Gail had always made me nervous, right up to the day her own uncle fired her for shoplifting. I couldn't believe he'd hired her again.

"Yeah." Her voice didn't give it away whether she remembered me or not. "I'm not working here or anything. No way. I had to fill in or something. What do you want?"

"Is my aunt there? Dotty?"

"Dotty!" I heard her scream. "Dotty! Telephone!" Somebody far from the phone must have said something, but I couldn't make it out. Then Gail said, "Oh yeah. I forgot." She came on the line again. "Dotty's not here."

"What? Why not?" Dotty never missed work.

"My uncle said she drove to Hamilton to pick up something for a basket."

"Hamilton?" Then I remembered. A women's missionary group at church was putting together food and gift baskets to send overseas. Dotty couldn't be part of the group because they met during the day, when she was working. But she was always running someplace to pick up something for somebody. "Did she say when she'd be back? Or was she going to come home after—?"

"Am I her secretary?" Gail asked.

"Thanks," I said, just as I heard the click of the receiver at the other end of the line.

I hung up and went back to B.C. "Listen, B.C.," I said, feeling better about the way he was sitting. His shoulders slumped, and his back wasn't so rigid. His eyes moved when I spoke to him. "Will you promise to stay right here if I go do chores?"

His head moved, and I took it for a nod yes.

"Good. Okay then. I'll be right back. And Dotty should be home soon. You stay here. Don't go anywhere."

I was pretty sure he'd be okay. B.C. can change moods fast, but it takes a lot out of him. I didn't think he'd be swinging back to high gear any time soon. Still, I ran most of the way to Horsefeathers.

The horses, bunched together by the barn, whinnied as I jogged up the lane. It took me a while to grain all 10 horses and turn them out in the right pastures. The whole time, I kept gazing down the lane toward the road, hoping help would show up from somewhere. Why was it that Maggie, Carla, and Jen were never there when I really needed them?

Orphan hung around after the others settled into their pastures. "Sorry, Girl," I told her, scratching under her mane. She stretched her neck and lifted her chin. Normally I stick around for an hour to spend time with my horse. We both unwind, usually by going for a ride in the back pastures.

Confused, Orphan and Misty watched as I headed home. When I turned down the lane, I heard Orphan's nicker. People talk about the good feeling of "coming home" after a hard day at school or at work. That's not how I feel when I come home. Instead, I get a fluttering at the back of my throat, a tightness in my chest, a tingling in my stomach, as I wonder what I'll find at home. The "coming home" feeling is what I sense when I walk into the barn at Horsefeathers.

No TV blaring, I told myself as I crossed the lawn. *That's a good sign.* But the phone was ringing. It kept ringing and ringing as I stepped to the porch. It kept ringing as I walked inside.

B.C. was sitting exactly where I'd left him. "B.C.! Get the phone!"

He didn't.

I grabbed the receiver in mid-ring. "Hello?"

"Brother! How many times do you gotta have it ring before you answer over there?"

"Tommy?" I asked, walking around the chair so I wouldn't pull the phone off the table.

"No. George Washington," he said, taking away my last ounce of doubt. Tommy Zucker is the same age as my brother, but he sounds 10 years older. Maybe it was having to make himself heard in a family of nine kids. Travis and Jen have the same confidence, but without Tommy's orneriness.

"What can I do for you, Tommy?" I asked.

"I want to talk to B.C.," Tommy said. "Is he home?"

"Yeah ..." I said slowly, eyeing my brother. I thought he was listening and watching out of the corner of his eye. What did we have to lose? "B.C., Tommy Zucker wants you."

He didn't answer. I stretched the phone as far as it would go and stuck the receiver to B.C.'s ear. His hand moved up and let me slide the receiver in.

I walked to the kitchen for a glass of water, but kept one ear tuned to the phone conversation. Only there wasn't any—not on B.C.'s end. He frowned, as if he were listening to Tommy. But he didn't make listening noises—no grunting, no *uh-huh*-ing.

I added my glass to the sink full of dishes. A *clunk* came from the living room, the sound of the phone hitting wood. I ran back just as B.C. banged out the screen door. The phone dangled off the arm of the couch. I picked it up.

"Tommy, are you still there?" I listened to

the crunch of B.C.'s bare feet as he climbed onto the roof. He'd be okay on the roof. It's where we both do a lot of our thinking. "Tommy?"

"Yeah, I'm still here. You better do something about your brother though," he said. "He's nuts."

"Don't say that, Tommy," I scolded. "What did you say to B.C.?"

"I didn't say nothing!" he protested. "It wasn't *my* idea to call him in the first place. Travis made me."

"You said *something* to him, Tommy." I tried to keep the anger, or the fear, out of my voice.

"I told him Travis signed up both of us for the King's Kamp thing. He didn't say anything back."

On Tommy's end, the phone clunked. Then Travis's voice came over the line. "Scoop? Is B.C. all right?"

I heard B.C. cross the roof above me and settle in the spot above the stairs. "I better go after him, Travis," I said. "B.C.'s pretty upset."

"I'm sorry, Scoop," Travis said, his voice so concerned I felt like I was going to give in and bawl like a baby. "Tommy didn't even try to tease B.C. Really. I was right here to make sure. I just thought it might be fun for B.C. if Tommy called him."

"It's not your fault, Travis," I said, swallowing the tears that wanted to come up. "Or

Tommy's. I don't know why B.C.'s acting this way." *How deep? How long?* "I have to go."

"Call me later," Travis said.

I hung up and joined B.C. on the roof. The shingles were hot. I couldn't imagine how B.C. had walked on them barefoot. He'd found the only spot that wouldn't burn us to sit down, under the overhanging oak. I had no idea what to say to him. Dotty would have known what to do. Dotty would have prayed.

Lord, I prayed, *help B.C. come out of it. At least don't let him go so deep he won't talk to me.* I hated that I hadn't thought to pray sooner. Dotty would have been talking to Jesus the whole time.

We sat in silence for a few minutes. Then B.C. whispered, "Tommy thinks I'm nuts."

"No he doesn't," I lied. Those had been Tommy's exact words.

"At camp," he said slowly, "Ms. Mansfield kept saying we were a team. All we needed was teamwork. But we *weren't* a team." He turned and looked straight at me. "Tommy Zucker said you told Travis to sign me back up at King's Kamp."

Tears leaked out of my eyes. I felt crushed with emotions. I was grateful that B.C. was talking in whole sentences. I was grateful that he was talking to *me,* instead of waiting for Dotty. But it hurt to know he thought I'd betrayed him.

"B.C., it's not what you think."

"Did he make it up?" B.C. turned big, black eyes on me.

I swallowed hard. "No. I did ask Travis to sign you up, but—"

"I won't go!" B.C. screamed. He stood up so suddenly, he lost his balance. His arms flew out at his sides, and for an instant I thought he was going to fly.

8

Don't, B.C.!" I cried, grabbing his ankle. He kicked one leg to make me let go. For a second, he tottered on the edge of the roof.

"You're not going to King's Kamp!" I screamed.

He stopped kicking and frowned down at me. His body turned to stone as he studied my face until he got what he needed. Then he sagged to the shingles as if his bones had dissolved.

As quickly and clearly as I could, I told B.C. about the plan Travis and I had to get riding students for the King's Kamp horses. I told my brother that I'd count on him to help me since he knew more about horses than the other boys. Little by little, he came around. "And that's why Travis signed you and Tommy up—just so we can call you King's Kamp students. All the lessons will be at Horsefeathers."

"So Tommy and me? We're the ones taking lessons? When do we start?"

It was great to see B.C. interested, maybe

even looking forward to something. It would have been horrible to have him end up disappointed. "B.C," I said, working my way to the willow tree because it's easier to climb down than the oak. "I'm going to call Travis back for a few details."

What if Travis couldn't get the other two students? What if that's what he wanted to talk to me about? What if I have to tell B.C. there won't be riding lessons?

I hurried down and dialed the Zuckers. Travis must have been waiting by the phone. "Hello?"

"Travis, it's Scoop."

"Is B.C. okay?" He sounded anxious.

"He's fine. He's even looking forward to riding lessons. Tell me he won't be disappointed, Travis. Tell me we're all set. Tell me we've got four students and the go-ahead from the camp."

"It went just like you said, Scoop," Travis said. "Mr. Rudd didn't take much convincing. He wanted Eric to ride all along. When I called Mrs. Miller, she said they'd changed their minds and were getting ready to call King's Kamp themselves. She sounded so worn down I had to feel sorry for them."

"Yes!" I shouted. "We're in!"

"Scoop, hold on a minute, will you? There's a slight hitch in our plans. The go-ahead came with a condition."

"What? What condition?" My stomach churned as I waited.

"We had to agree to take on help, someone from the camp to look after the interests of the kids."

"That's not so bad," I said, relieved.

"Scoop," Travis said. I heard his sigh over the telephone wire. "The *helper* ... it's Ms. Mansfield."

After Travis and I hung up, I sat staring at the blank TV the way B.C. had. Ms. Mansfield and I had gotten off to a bad start. How could I do my job with her breathing down my neck?

"Scoop?" B.C. sat beside me on the couch. "Is everything okay?"

I pulled myself together and forced a Maggie-37 enthusiasm I didn't feel. "It's all set, B.C. Travis got two more riders, so it's four boys for four horses."

B.C. frowned. "Who? Which boys?"

I tried to remember the names Travis had given me. "Eric ... Eric Rudd." I remembered because of what Travis said about his face being red. I'd already decided to match him with the Chestnut gelding I was working with, Red—not because of his color, but because they were both scared.

B.C. seemed to relax. "I know Eric. He's a cry baby."

"That's not very nice, B.C.," I said.

B.C. looked sheepish. "That's what David calls him."

"I'll bet Eric doesn't like it, you think? Maybe you can help Eric not be scared of the horses."

B.C. looked up at me. "I could. If he's a-scared, like he was a-scared to play football, I can teach him horses aren't scary."

"That would be great, B.C." I tried to remember the other boy's name. "Miller. That's the other boy who wants to take lessons at Horsefeathers."

"I don't know any boy named Miller," B.C. said.

"That's his last name. Travis didn't know the first name." I decided it might be best not to mention Ms. Mansfield for the time being.

By the time Dotty got back from her errand, B.C. and I had already stuffed ourselves with peanut butter and stale crackers. I called Maggie to tell her the good news about the boys signing up, but she already knew. Jen was spending the night.

~~~~~~~~~~~~~~~~~~~~~~~~~~~~

The next morning at church Jen and Carla were standing on the steps laughing about something. Carla went in just as I got there.

"Scoop!" Jen hollered when she spotted me. I joined her on the step as people flowed past us. "Wait until you hear what Maggie and I came up with! We were up all night working on it. We've got at least three of the riding lessons planned out. I'm still doing research on a couple of things I can pass along to the boys—facts and theories and strategies. Maggie's practicing a great introduction for the camp kids, kind of a welcome, an opening show. It'll be great when she finishes."

I nodded, all the while disagreeing with every word Jen said. Why did we need facts and theories? We sure didn't need one of Maggie's show routines to open our riding camp. And why hadn't they included me in their little overnight?

Dotty and B.C. trailed up the stairs. "Morning, Jen!" Dotty said. "Ain't you looking prettier than ever!"

I hadn't noticed until Dotty said something, but Jen did look nice. She wore a sleeveless, pale blue dress with tiny buttons all the way down and a belt that showed how small her waist was. Her long blond hair had been combed to the side, with curly wisps framing her oval face. Jen's ivory skin is whiter than anybody's I know, but on her it looks perfect. Behind her wire-rimmed glasses her eyes were as blue as spring sky.

Since Dotty was working downstairs in child care, I had to take care of B.C. during the service.

"I want to sit with Tommy and the Zuckers!" B.C. insisted, as I pulled him to our pew.

"No you don't," I whispered, pushing him in and sliding next to him.

"Do too!" he said, way too loud for church. The organ started playing.

Mrs. Powers turned around from the pew ahead of us. The bouquet of flowers sticking out of her pink straw hat matched the flowers on her dress. B.C. calls her the Hat Lady. "Morning, you two," she said. "B.C., I am so pleased you're sitting behind me. I love to hear you sing." She winked at me.

B.C. didn't say anything, but he stopped fighting me to go sit by Tommy. And during the hymns, he sang extra loud.

Pastor Dan started the announcements with King's Kamp news. "The sponsors of the camp wanted me to pass along their thanks to the Daltons for donating horses."

I didn't turn around the way most people did to smile at the Daltons, who were seated two pews behind us. Stephen and his girlfriend, Ursula, sat by themselves in the pew directly behind me. Stephen leaned forward and whispered, "Don't worry, Sarah. Nobody expects this to work out. But we'll still get our money out of the deal. That slaughterhouse runs a good business."

I pretended not to hear Stephen, but I felt like I might throw up.

"Lessons begin at Horsefeathers Stable a

week from Monday," the pastor continued. "Transportation will be provided for the boys to and from King's Kamp for lessons Monday, Wednesday, and Friday the next two weeks. We can still use volunteers to help us get the barn ready.

"And speaking of volunteers ..." Pastor Dan pointed at the Hat Lady. "Mrs. Powers, would you stand up, please?" She did, and her flowers seem to grow as she rose in front of us. "The church would like to thank you for the good work you've put in on our missionary baskets. They're wonderful, and I'm sure our missionaries will think so too!"

"Well," said the Hat Lady, "I certainly did not put those baskets together by myself." She glanced over the congregation. "Irma, Elsie, Donna, Helen, stand up with me."

One by one, the Women's Missionary Society got to their feet and reluctantly accepted our applause. Nobody mentioned all the trips Dotty had made to get them the stuff they needed in the first place. To be fair, I had to admit that the Hat Lady might have thought of it if Dotty hadn't been in the basement with the infants and toddlers.

~~~~~~~~~~~~~~~~~~~~~~~~~~~~~

Sunday afternoon is my favorite time in the whole week. No matter how crazy things get, I know I'll have Sunday. Instead of working the horses at Horsefeathers, I socialize with them. Later in the afternoon, I ride Orphan. I needed that ride more than ever.

It was nearing sunset when Orphan and I cantered to the pond to cool off. Orphan waded up to her knees, stirring up the muddy water. Then she leaned forward and glided into a swim. I hugged her neck and let my legs float behind me. We were weightless, moving through the cool water as one.

As Orphan climbed the bank up from the pond, I held onto her mane. I wanted to hold on to the pond-peace too, but it evaporated as quickly as the water beads on my arms. I didn't want to think about the slaughterhouse. I didn't want to think about Jen and Maggie and their plans for the Horsefeathers' lessons. What were they thinking anyway? The last thing I wanted to do was to turn Horsefeathers into a fancy riding academy.

During the next week, I spent every minute working the King's Kamp horses, as we'd started calling them. Since I didn't want to step on anybody's toes, I tried to ride the other horses when nobody was around. But a couple of times I got caught. On Monday Jen showed up to ride Babe when I was loping her around the pasture.

Maggie found me putting Dusty through his paces on Wednesday. But I waited until Carla had finished her English-equitation workout on

Bruiser before I dared work *him*. Little by little, I got to know each horse and trusted that they'd all do just fine for our students.

I'd asked everybody to show up for practice at 10:00 Saturday morning so we could get the horses used to sharing the arena. Travis brought Jen early. During the week, he and Jen had replaced saddle straps and girths, and the saddles looked great.

While we were putting the identical saddles on Babe and Red, Carla Buckingham walked up. She wore a short-sleeved cotton shirt tucked into her crisp blue jeans. Her dark hair was pulled back in a short pony tail that shined in the sunlight.

"Hey, Carla!" Travis called. "You've got Bruiser, right? I'll pull out his saddle for you."

Travis walked off, and I couldn't help feeling smug. At least now Bruiser would get the Western workout he needed.

"How's Babe coming along?" Carla asked Jen, who was trying to tighten the saddle girth. I saw the tip of Babe's tongue sticking out from her mouth. The Palomino was holding her breath to make sure Jen couldn't get the cinch too tight.

"I haven't had any problems with Babe all week," Jen answered. "I think Travis and Scoop conspired to give me the gentlest horse. How about you and Bruiser?"

"No problems here," Carla said.

I wondered. I'd only seen her ride him twice.

Jen and I rode Babe and Red while Travis helped Carla saddle Bruiser. Our horses moved easily at a trot, Red taking the gait at harness speed and Babe falling into a slow jog trot. As Red and I moved past them on the inside, I noticed something thrown over Jen's saddle horn. "What's that, Jen?"

"This?" She sped up to keep pace with Red and me. "It's a lariat. I've been practicing for Monday's opening lesson." She took the wound rope from the saddle horn and held the noose end in her right hand, the reins in her left. "Wait till you see what Maggie taught me." Jen raised her arm above her head and twirled the lariat.

The second Jen swung the rope, my horse stiffened. His forelegs dug into the dirt. He stopped so short, I nearly went over his head.

"Scoop! What are you doing?" Jen shouted, as she and Babe continued around the arena in front of us.

Even though he was shaking with fear, Red didn't throw a fit or try to run away or buck me off. He just balked, refusing to go forward. "Come on, Red," I said, willing him to go. He refused. I tried turning him to the left, then to the right.

"Jen, put the rope away!" I yelled across the paddock.

"What?" she shouted back. She stood in the stirrups and stared over at me.

Carla was riding out of the barn on Bruiser. I saw her urge the Pinto into the paddock. She had no way of knowing that Jen and Babe were rounding the corner and heading straight for her.

"Stop, Carla!" I screamed, waving my arms at her.

Carla didn't stop. She squinted at me from the shadow of the barn. Bruiser squirmed under the silver-studded saddle. He pranced and tossed his head.

I turned to Jen, who hadn't slowed Babe. If anything, they were jogging faster. Faster and straight for Carla and Bruiser.

I froze. Jen and Carla didn't see each other. They were both looking at me.

Then it happened. Jen screamed, but she was too late to stop her horse. Babe rammed into Bruiser, hitting him broadside.

9

Dust flew. Horses squealed. Jen and Carla screamed.

I jumped off Red. "Are you all right?" I cried, racing to the tangle of horses and girls. Both riders had managed to stay on, although Carla had lost both stirrups.

Travis came racing out of the barn. "Jen! Are you okay? Is she okay?" He ran straight at Jen and Babe, then tried to grab his sister to lift her down.

"Back off, Travis!" Jen shouted. "I'm fine. Carla, are you all right? I didn't see you. I am so sorry."

Carla acted like she didn't hear Jen. She was leaning down to put her boot back in the stirrup. Bruiser wouldn't stand still for it. He side-stepped, backed up, stamped his hoof.

But Babe was the one I was worried about. I checked her head and chest. I was pretty sure neither horse had been hurt. But the Palomino was trembling, her eyes wide and watery.

Stroking her neck, I slid my finger to her

throat and felt her pulse. It was as rapid as a race horse's. Her ears twitched, rotating toward Bruiser, then to the pasture, then to Red.

"You sure you're all right, Jen?" Travis asked, his hand on her knee, ready to keep her from falling. "Your glasses!"

Jen squinted and felt her face, but her glasses weren't there.

Carefully, I stepped around Babe, looking in the dirt. Retracing Babe's steps, I surveyed the path until I saw the glasses upside down in a pile of dust, the gold wires sticking up. "Found 'em!" I cried.

Travis took the glasses from me and blew on the lenses. He shook his head. "The lenses aren't broken, Jen." One of the ear pieces was twisted in the middle, making a letter *L*. Travis tried to twist it back. "We'll get you new frames. I can't believe the lenses didn't break. Talk about miracles ..."

When Travis handed the glasses to his sister, it was pretty clear that he was the only one who considered all this miraculous. Jen frowned at the twisted frames. Carla didn't say anything, but she looked angry.

I walked back to Red, who might as well have been glued to the spot. Even thinking the word *glue* brought nightmare visions of slaughterhouses to my brain. I pushed them away. It took some talking before Red let me lead him away and mount. Forcing him to move just didn't work. I had to talk him out of it.

The three of us rode at a walk, spacing ourselves, keeping yards apart, while Travis kept a close eye out from the center of the arena. Babe settled down pretty quickly. But Bruiser never did give Carla a clean ride. His walk was stiff, and he broke stride when we loped.

"Thanks a lot for waiting!" Maggie 37 climbed over the paddock fence and scurried to the center of the arena, next to Travis. Everything she wore, from her capris to her hair ribbons, was bright purple. "Jen, I told you not to let the fun start without me."

"You're an hour late, Maggie!" I said, madder than I should have been.

"I told Jen I had practice," she said defensively.

"What was it this time?" I asked. "Voice lessons or theater practice? Or maybe piano or violin? Or ballet? How about tiddley winks? Anything except horse lessons." I knew I was taking my frustrations out on Maggie.

But it just wasn't fair. *Why can't she care enough about Horsefeathers to be here? Everybody expects me to take care of the hard stuff. Where were they when I cleaned the extra stalls? Where were they when I needed help with night chores so I could stay with B.C.?*

"I'll get Dusty." Maggie walked to the pasture. Nobody said anything.

Nobody said much the rest of the practice. Maggie and Dusty put in a horrible workout, with Dusty pokey and Maggie in a rush. I wanted to tell her to slow down and be patient with her horse. Dusty didn't have ballet and voice lessons to run off to, so he was in no hurry. But Maggie avoided me.

At Travis's suggestion, we agreed to show up at Horsefeathers at 9 a.m. Monday, an hour before the boys were scheduled to arrive from King's Kamp. I wanted to tell Jen and Maggie that it wouldn't work to greet the boys with an opening show the way they'd planned. We only had six lessons with the King's Kamp boys, and I didn't want to waste the first one. But I was afraid to say so now.

Maggie was the first to leave. Jen followed her, and Travis drove them both home. Ray came by for Carla. And of course, I was left to muck the stalls by myself.

Monday morning I got up while it was still dark. At least we didn't have to worry about getting rained out. Already, or *still*, heat surrounded everything like a second skin, inside and out. I was surprised to see a light glowing from the kitchen when I came downstairs.

"Dotty? What are you doing up already?"

Dotty was hunched over a pile of envelopes, her tongue stuck out to seal the one in her hand. "Scoop! You liked to give me a heart attack! I didn't hear you." She licked the flap and pushed it down with the heel of her hand, then dropped it into a box of sealed envelopes.

Grabbing another unsealed envelope, she said, "I shoulda did these here ones last night, but I got to talking with Jack Jackson. Did you know his son and daughter-in-law stuck that poor man in the Kennsington nursing home? They ain't went to see him in nigh onto two months. Lord, help Mr. Jackson to know You is ... *slurp* ... his real home." In the middle of her prayer, she licked another envelope.

"What are you mailing out?" I asked, pouring myself a glass of juice, smelling it first.

"You know how Pastor Dan, he gets hisself into a tizzy if he's got to ask the church to come up with money? So the money committee come up with the idea to write about it instead. They's sending this letter to all folks that's ever come to our church. Some of it, they gonna use to get them horses food and fix up that barn at King's Kamp."

"And *you* have to send the letters out?" It would be just like the errands for the missionaries. Nobody would care.

"I don't mind. Makes me feel part of things—like if I didn't lick this here glue, there couldn't be no camp for boys." I watched Dotty finish the stack as I downed half a bowl of Tastee-O's. All I could think as I watched her *lift, lick, pound, drop,* was that if the Horsefeathers riding clinic didn't work, we wouldn't need the money they were asking for. King's Kamp wouldn't need a barn, and the horses wouldn't need food. Money wouldn't help us if we had to give back the horses to Ralph Dalton.

I got to Horsefeathers before the horses had time to think about breakfast. Graining them early though would help their performance. I'd had time to think about what we needed to do in our first lesson with the King's Kamp kids. All I wanted to achieve in our first hour was to lessen any fears of horses. The boys needed to get to know the horses. I wanted each boy to bond with the horse I'd assigned him.

Horses need to *join up* with their riders or handlers. In the horse business, *joining up* has come to mean forming a team. There's a moment when a horse decides for himself that he's better off working *with* people than against them. If we could cause the horses to join up with our students, lessons would go a whole lot easier.

B. C. was the first to show at Horsefeathers. He tried to help me brush each horse as the sun rose higher and hotter by the minute.

"I'll probably have to show the other boys how to ride good," he said as he raked his fingers through Babe's white forelock. "I'll bet they've never even been on a horse—not like me."

Actually, B.C. hadn't ridden much. I'd let him ride double with me on Orphan a couple of times, and by himself once or twice. His colt, Misty, was still a year-and-a-half or more away from riding age.

Orphan whinnied at me from her ringside seat on the other side of the paddock. Misty followed suit and nickered. "You can show the other boys your colt," I suggested. "And you can show them what it's like not to be afraid of horses."

Travis dropped Jen off at about 8:30, then drove away. I'd finished brushing all of the horses and started picking out Red's hooves when Jen walked into the barn.

"Hey, Jen," I called from Red's stall. "Where's Travis?"

Jen yawned and strolled over. "Travis told Ms. Mansfield he'd play chauffeur and drive the boys to Horsefeathers. He's driven the camp van lots of times for them over the summer. We were hoping Ms. Mansfield would take Travis up on his offer, and then stay at King's Kamp herself."

I finished Red's left forefoot and back foot and moved to the other side. "Did it work?" I asked her.

"No it didn't," Jen answered. "Ms. Mansfield said Travis could drive, and she would keep an eye on the boys during the ride over. Travis took Tommy with him."

Jen got another hoof pick and joined Babe in the stall next to me. I heard the scrape of the iron tool on hoof. I hoped she wouldn't miss Babe's frog and the V-groove of the inner hoof.

When I was done with Red, I said, "Jen, you want me to finish off Babe for you?"

"I'm doing fine, Scoop," she answered.

I watched her lean into Babe to get her to give up her back hoof. "You know," I said, straining to get a better look, "I've been thinking a lot about which boy should get which horse. The kid named Eric Rudd, I guess he's pretty scared to take riding lessons."

Jen moved to Babe's right side and picked up the back foot. I would have gone up to the foreleg first. "Eric? The red-headed kid?" Jen asked.

"Right. I thought he'd be a good match to Red, the Chestnut I've been looking after. Red's got some fear too."

"So they can be frightened together. Is that what you're thinking?" Jen didn't sound like she thought it was such a good idea.

"Well, yeah," I said. "I've spent the most time with Red, and I know he's a safe ride. And maybe Eric will feel safer, like he's got to look out for the frightened horse. I'd like to see B.C. on Dusty. B.C. wouldn't mind how big Dusty is, and the old work horse can be trusted to go easy, even if my brother gets hyper. Tommy would probably like Bruiser. I don't think he'd be scared if the Pinto starts that sidestepping business."

Jen moved to the last hoof. Babe raised her foot in anticipation before Jen even got settled. "You've got it all worked out, don't you, Scoop?"

She was standing too close to Babe. Her foot was in the exact spot Babe's had been before Jen lifted it. "Better move your foot, or you're going to get stepped on," I said. "Where was I? Okay. We don't know anything about the other boy, the Miller kid," I said. "So he'd be a good one to put on Babe. She's so reliable. And you could—"

We were interrupted by Carla and Maggie. I was pretty sure they hadn't come together, but they walked in at the same time. They both wore jeans, but Maggie had matched hers with a blue denim short-sleeved shirt. Her hair had been braided in dozens of tiny braids that she'd pulled into a high ponytail.

"And the time is ..." Maggie paused dramatically. "Ten till nine. *Drum roll, please!*"

We exchanged polite good mornings, then went about the work of preparing the horses.

"Where's Travis, Jen?" Maggie asked, as she put old Dusty in the cross-ties and started brushing him. I'd already groomed Dusty, but I kept my mouth shut.

"Travis is driving the boys here ... *and* Ms.

Mansfield," Jen answered. "Maybe he can soften her up for us."

"If anyone can do it, Travis can," Maggie said dreamily. She'd never kept her crush on Jen's big brother a secret.

Well before 10:00, we had the horses saddled and bridled. Ray stopped by and went straight to Carla, never to be seen again. They huddled back in the corner of the barn as if the rest of us weren't there. I didn't even know Ray had left until I saw him at the end of the lane.

Twice I almost apologized to Maggie for blowing up at her Saturday. But *she* made no move to apologize to *me* for not doing her share of the work all week.

"They're here!" B.C. yelled, jumping from the loft and darting past us to the paddock.

I glanced at Maggie, and she quickly looked away. I hated the tension between us, but I had more pressing worries. A white van with *King's Kamp* printed on the side in green letters was creeping up the drive. Through the open van windows, we could hear the anguished cries of Ms. Mansfield.

10

S top that this instant!" yelled Ms. Mansfield. "Or I will tell Travis to drive straight back to King's Kamp!" It was amazing how well her voice carried from the van, through the paddock, to my ears.

"Line up the horses," I whispered. I backed Red in next to Jen and Babe, and we waved.

Maggie tugged on Dusty's reins to get her near us. "One of you has to hold Dusty so I can get Moby," she said, still pulling the giant Blue Roan.

"Why?" I asked, one eye on the van.

"For the show!" Maggie exclaimed.

"Maggie," I said, intent on the van's back door that opened before Travis had time to turn off the ignition. Two boys tumbled out, scuffling and elbowing each other. One looked like Tommy, with the Zucker blond hair. "Look, I didn't want to say so earlier, but that show thing just isn't going to work."

"What?" Maggie cried. She made a face to Jen. Both of them frowned at me.

"We don't have time to watch tricks. Not today anyway." I should have told them earlier. But it was their own fault for planning everything without even talking to me about it. "Don't be mad," I begged, staring toward the white van. "It's the boys who need to do the riding."

Next to the van, Tommy Zucker and a taller, skinnier boy were getting into a shoving match.

"So what are you saying?" Jen asked. "You want the boys to put on the show?"

"Hmm?" I was barely listening to them. I waved again. Behind Red, Bruiser complained, snorting and stamping his hooves. Carla walked him in circles to calm him down. She circled too close. Bruiser nipped Red's rump. Red squealed.

"It's an idea, Maggie," Jen said. "Instead of putting on the show ourselves, we could teach the boys to put on a show for their parents. It would be great advertising for Horsefeathers. Moby could still perform, of course."

Tommy Zucker and the tall kid raced to the fence. The tall kid got there first and climbed over in two steps. He was skinny, but big-boned, rugged, with a scowl that made him look fierce. His only attractive feature was an amazing head of coal black hair combed neatly to the side.

"I like it," Maggie said. I'd forgotten what they were talking about. I didn't know what she liked, and I didn't much care. "We'll do it, Jen," she said. She wasn't talking to me anyway.

Travis was pulling out the third boy by his elbow. Even without spotting the kid's red hair, I would have guessed that he was Eric Rudd.

"Yuk!" said the tall kid, running up to Red and checking him out. "What a broken-down saddle!"

"Welcome to Horsefeathers ... Mr. Miller, is it?" I said, sticking out my hand for him to shake. He didn't. "I'm Scoop."

His ribs showed through his white T-shirt, but he was no weakling. He eyed the Palomino Babe, then passed by her. He laughed at the big Blue Roan, Dusty, as he ran past him, not even bothering to stop.

"That's the one!" he shouted, pushing between Babe and Red to get to Carla and Bruiser. "I'll take this horse."

"No, not that one," I called after him. I pointed out Babe. "*This* is the horse we've got for you. Look at this beautiful Palomino."

"This one has the best saddle, and I want it!" he yelled, touching the silver spangles on Bruiser's black stirrups.

"Scoop!" Travis waved for me to come and get the terrified Eric Rudd. We guided Eric to slip through the boards and into the paddock, but it would take more than guiding to get Eric to come any closer to the horses.

A scream came from the barn. Right away I recognized B.C.'s cry. I ran to B.C., hoping I could reach him before he scared every horse in three counties.

"B.C.!" I cried, squatting beside him and covering his mouth with my hand. "Stop it!"

When he did, I removed my hand.

"You lied! You lied! You didn't tell me who was really coming!" He yelled as loudly as he'd screamed.

"I did not lie, B.C.!" I yelled back.

"You did too!" he shouted. He pointed at the Miller kid. "That's *him!* That's David! *The* David! The David who dunks me in toilets! Make him go back to King's Kamp!"

David Miller? I thought, putting the pieces together. "I won't let him hurt you, B.C.," I promised.

I peeked over my shoulder as Tommy Zucker charged at Dusty. He almost knocked over Eric Rudd, who stood in his way. Eric burst into tears.

"I get this monster horse!" Tommy yelled. He lunged at poor Dusty, trying to jump on the horse's back.

I dragged B.C. over to the pack. He broke free and ran behind Maggie, who was trying to get Tommy Zucker to quit ramming the horse. Eric's sobs were louder than my brother's scream.

"Come on, Eric," I said, leading him to Red. "See this great horse? This one is for *you*."

Eric doubled his volume, spitting out cries that would shame a police siren. Red trembled.

David Miller covered his ears. He turned to B.C. "Why aren't *you* crying, cry baby? Then he wheeled on Tommy Zucker. "*My* horse is better than *your* horse!"

"Is not!" Tommy exclaimed.

"Is so!" David insisted.

"Is not!"

"Is so!"

"No!" I shouted. "You've both got the wrong horse! B.C. gets the big horse. David, this Palomino is yours. Tommy gets the Pinto."

"No!" David shouted. Before I knew what was happening, David jumped on Tommy, knocking him to the dirt. "*I'm* taking the one with the silver saddle!" he screamed. "And you're not getting it!"

Tommy fought back. They rolled across the paddock, stirring up clouds of dust. Eric bawled louder. B.C. hid behind Maggie. Bruiser broke loose from Carla and charged Red. He bit the poor gelding, sending him squealing around the paddock in a riderless race.

I looked on, helpless and in shock. And just when I thought things couldn't possibly get worse, they did. Ms. Mansfield entered the arena.

"What kind of a zoo are you running here? I told Mr. Dalton this would never work. I don't know why I agreed to go along with this charade." Ms. Mansfield stared down at us as if we were cockroaches ... and she was the exterminator. "Tommy! David! Stop fighting this minute!"

They scrambled to their feet. Tommy brushed off paddock dust. David smoothed down his black hair.

"That kid tried to take my horse!" David shouted. "And then he messed up my hair." He shook his fist at Tommy Zucker.

"Did not!" Tommy shouted.

"Did too!"

"Did not!"

"Did too!"

"Tommy! David! Enough!" Travis cried. He tried to bring back the winning Travis smile, but it wouldn't come. "Usually, Horsefeathers Stable is nothing like this. Really, it's not, Ms. Mansfield," he said. His arms were filled with four white helmets. He reached for his brother Tommy and dropped one of the helmets. When he leaned down to pick it up, he dropped the others.

"No way I'm wearing one of those on *my* hair!" David declared. The kid definitely had a thing about his hair.

"There may indeed be no need, David," Ms. Mansfield said coldly. "I didn't really believe this would work out for King's Kamp. It would appear that I was correct. Perhaps we should just call the whole thing off."

"Horsefeathers, Mr. Mansfield!" I exclaimed, visualizing the horses being loaded up and sent off to the slaughterhouse.

David laughed and pointed at the woman. Then Tommy pointed too. He doubled over with laughter.

I looked helplessly to Travis, whose eyes filled with pity for me.

Jen leaned in and whispered, "Scoop, you called her *Mister* Mansfield."

"N-no," I stammered. "I-I—I didn't mean—"

Ms. Mansfield's upper lip curled, and her nostrils widened so far I could see little black hairs inside. "Tommy! David! Eric!" She didn't move her gaze from me, not even when the three boys scurried in front of her and formed ranks. "Boys, you can go back to the van now. Your riding lessons are over!"

11

Aw, man!" David Miller kicked up dust. "I knew we wouldn't get no riding lessons. It was all a big lie."

"Will y'all excuse me a little minute?" Maggie 37 stepped up to Ms. Mansfield and took her hand. "You must be Ms. Mansfield." Her southern accent oozed.

Ms. Mansfield didn't smile back, but she allowed the Southern Maggie to shake her hand.

"Everyone has told me so much about you, Ms. Mansfield, and all you've accomplished in the social work field. Only I thought you'd be older, surely! And here you are—not much older than little ol' me!"

Ms. Mansfield frowned at her as if Maggie 37 had just dropped from a space ship.

"Where *are* my manners? I declare, having you here and in person has put me beside myself!" Maggie continued. "I am Maggie 37 Blue." Maggie curtsied. "I believe you've met Sarah Coop, better known as Scoop."

I smiled weakly and nodded.

Maggie did a graceful turn, extending her arm in Jen's direction. "I don't know if you've had the pleasure of meeting Travis's sister Jen. And behind her is Carla Buckingham. You have no doubt heard of the Edward Buckinghams."

"Ah yes?" said Ms. Mansfield, stretching her long neck to see one of the famous Buckinghams in person.

"On behalf of all of us here at Horsefeathers, I have the honor of welcoming you to our stable," Maggie said. "We so much appreciate your generosity in giving your time to come visit us with these poor, unfortunate boys."

"Hey!" David objected. "I'm not poor and unfortunate!"

Maggie ignored David and kept buttering up Ms. Mansfield. "We look forward to learning all we can from you, Ms. Mansfield."

Maggie dropped Dusty's reins. That horse wasn't going anywhere. "If y'all would be so kind as to follow me ..."

"Well, I don't know ..." Ms. Mansfield showed signs of weakening. She relaxed her shoulders and sized up the horses.

"I have so looked forward to this moment," Maggie said, her hand gently resting on Ms. Mansfield's broad back. "Now, you wouldn't want to disappoint a girl, would you?" Maggie guided her skillfully away, toward the barn.

"I haven't told many people this," Maggie

said, as if they were co-conspirators. "But my dream is that one day I too can become a social worker."

Right. Social, maybe. Worker, never—unless you call acting work.

But from the intent expression on Ms. Mansfield's face as Maggie led her away, the woman was totally buying into the performance. Maggie showed her to a lawn chair I'd never seen before. It was set against the barn, in full view of the paddock, but out of the way.

"Y'all will have the best seat in the house!" Maggie exclaimed. "The only shady seat—that's for sure."

They actually chuckled together. Then the mesmerized Ms. Mansfield took her assigned seat. Maggie 37 Brown, Orange, or Purple, can talk the eyelashes off a snake. She left the woman smiling and came back to turn her charms on the boys.

"So," Maggie said, every eye on her, "what do you say we check out the horses?"

"I'm riding this one!" David said, pointing to the Pinto Bruiser. "I get the best saddle!"

"Well, well," said Maggie. "That's a mighty fine horse *and* saddle, all right."

"Actually, David," I said, nudging Jen to lead Babe closer to David, "*this* is the horse I picked out for you. Her name is Babe. Isn't she pretty? And she rides so well."

"Yeah?" David said. "That's just great. *You* ride her. I already have a horse. Besides, that one looks like it's crying. Give it to one of the cry babies. Get it? *Babe*? Cry *Baby*?"

"No, David. You see, the Pinto here, Bruiser, is Tommy's mount for our riding lessons," I explained.

"I'd like to see him try!" David shouted, glaring at Tommy.

Tommy threw a sideways glance at David. Maybe B.C. had been right about David Miller. Even Tommy Zucker was thinking twice before taking the horse David wanted. "Nah," Tommy said, trying to reach Dusty's mane. "*This* is my horse. He's the biggest. I want the biggest horse."

"Tommy," I reasoned, "B.C. will be riding Dusty."

"No he won't!" Tommy shouted. "That's not fair! *I* said I wanted the big horse first!"

"Scoop," Jen said, "let Tommy have Dusty." She turned to my brother, who was hiding behind me. "B.C., why don't you come over and take Babe? I've been riding her this week, and I think you and Babe could be great friends."

Carla distracted David, who was trying to get his foot in Bruiser's stirrup, the *wrong* stirrup, on the poor horse's right side. "Here, David," Carla said. "Stroke Bruiser on his neck. He likes that."

Bruiser *didn't* like being touched. I knew that.

"So that's it, then?" Maggie said, as Tommy settled in next to her and reached up to Dusty's neck to pet him. "Eric, how are you and Red getting along?"

Eric shrugged. At least *he* had the right horse.

I wasn't sure how it had happened, but I had lost control of the horse clinic already.

"Boys, you need to stand on the left side of your horse," said Maggie 37. "We always mount from the left side."

"Why?" David asked, not committing himself to move yet. "I want to get on from the right side. I'm right-handed."

"That's a good question, David," I said, hearing my old fourth-grade teacher's words coming out of my mouth. "A good question deserves a good answer. We'll come back to it when we have more time."

"Whatever," David said.

"Actually, riders," Jen said, "David brings up a fascinating fact of history. Mounting from the left side of the horse is a habit brought down to us from the days of chivalry in France and England. The knight swung himself into the saddle from the left side of the horse to keep his right arm, his sword hand, free. It wasn't until—"

"Thanks, Jen," I said, interrupting her

before she launched into the history of the sword. "But we're not ready to mount yet ... from either side." I laughed weakly, but no one joined in. "There are a lot of things we need to learn before mounting. Mounting and dismounting are the two most dangerous skills a rider learns."

"*I'm* not afraid to mount!" declared David Miller, sticking his foot back in the stirrup. "I want a sword!"

"Don't forget their helmets!" Ms. Mansfield yelled from her shady seat. I'd almost forgotten that she was still there spying on us.

Travis had set the helmets on the ground by the gate. He pointed at the white pile. "We won't forget!" he shouted to her.

It was time for me to step up and regain control before everything got out of hand. "Let's start slowly," I suggested. "Boys, stand by your horses, just to the left side of the head."

I nodded for Travis to help Eric with Red, while I walked from horse to horse. Carla got David to stand where I wanted him to. I just hoped she could control the bully horse *and* the bully boy.

"Good," I said, when they all had their places. "See how big your horse's eyes are? They help him see things almost all the way around him—except directly in front and back. So don't stand right in front or right in back of your horse because you might frighten him."

Eric Rudd jumped out of the way. Tommy and David both moved directly in front of their horses. Carla and Maggie tugged them back.

"Go on and pet your darlings!" Maggie shouted.

David reached out and rubbed Bruiser's muzzle. Bruiser's ears went back.

"Don't pet him on the nose," I said quickly. "He might think your hand's a carrot and bite it." I heard Eric gasp. "Start out with long strokes under his mane. It will be up to you to discover where your horse likes you to pet him the best. Talk to your horse."

"Hey, Bruiser!" David screamed. "Let's race!"

"Talk softly," I said. "Horses have much better hearing than you do. And better smell too."

"Not this horse," Tommy said, holding his nose. "He smells gross!"

Carla did a good job keeping David under control. Even when he made fun of the way she talked, she didn't retreat or let it make her mad.

"What you want," I told the boys, "is to get your horse to *join up* with you."

"Join your stupid Horsefeathers club?" Tommy asked.

"Tommy!" Jen scolded.

"No," I said, trying to think of the best way to explain the process. "You and your horse need to become a team."

"Ugh!" All four of the boys groaned.

I remembered what B.C. had said about Ms. Mansfield's teamwork lectures at King's Kamp. Apparently, B.C. hadn't been the only one to have his fill of teamwork pep talks. "Sorry," I said. "We'll stick with *joining up* and just hope that you *and* your horse will figure it out by the time we're done."

It wasn't easy, but I got all the way through instructions on leading a horse. "Now, let's see what you've learned," I said. "Let's lead our horses. Fall in behind Eric and Red."

Eric shook his head and dropped Red's reins. I ran over and picked them up from the dirt. "Okay. Watch how Eric and I do it." Eric made me stand next to Red, while he stayed three feet on the other side of me.

"Don't forget," I called back to them. "Stand at your horse's left shoulder. Don't grab or rush. Take the reins in your right hand, just below the bit. Let the ends of the reins pass through your left hand. *Don't* wrap the reins around your hands ever! Face forward. Now, step out slowly. Use your horse's name and say 'Walk on.'"

Behind me several voices mumbled "Walk on," and one yelled, "Run!" Dusty took some maneuvering by Maggie, but finally they were all in motion. I glanced over my shoulder at the mini-parade of horses behind me. *Not bad. Not bad at all for my first official riding lesson.*

The third time we completed our circle, leading horses around the arena, Ms. Mansfield was waiting for us. "Time to go," she said.

"Wait a minute!" Tommy cried. "We didn't even get on the dumb horses!"

"This is so stupid!" David yelled, throwing down Bruiser's reins and stomping on them. "Some riding lesson. We didn't even ride! I'm not coming back here."

"Me neither!" said Tommy Zucker.

"Me too," said Eric.

"Me too," B.C. said.

Great! It was the first thing they'd agreed on all day, probably all camp. "But—" I tried to think how I could convince them. They *had* to come back.

Maggie took over. "Well y'all, that's too bad," she said, taking out her rubber band and freeing her braids. "That's a shame—about you fellas not coming back for the show."

I glanced over at Maggie. There wasn't going to be any show. "Maggie, I told you—"

"Who wants to see a dumb show?" David said.

"What?" Maggie turned wide eyes at David. "Oh, I thought your relatives would. Parents generally like that sort of thing, you know."

"Huh?" David frowned at Maggie. "*My* parents don't want to see any dumb stupid horse show. Why would they want to see some cry baby show with horses?"

"Maybe y'all are right," Maggie drawled. "I guess I just thought they would. I know *my* mother would *love* to see a show if *I* were starring in it. That's all."

"What do you mean 'starring' in the show?" asked Tommy, sounding a lot more interested.

Jen got in on the act. "Never mind, Tommy. Of course, Mom and Dad will be awfully disappointed. They were looking forward to seeing you perform on horseback after the lessons and all."

"You mean *we're* going to put on a show with the horses?" Tommy asked.

"That was the plan," Maggie said. "But I guess if you're not coming back to Horsefeathers, we can always—"

"*I* didn't say I wasn't coming back," Tommy said. "*David* said *he* wasn't coming back. I'm coming back. I'll star in the show."

"*I* know how to ride already," B.C. said. "I can put on a horse show."

"No way!" David yelled. "*I'm* the one with the fancy saddle. *I* should be the star."

The boys, still arguing over who would be the star of the show, left the paddock with Ms. Mansfield. I could still hear them arguing as they climbed into the van. Eric didn't join the argument, but at least he didn't cry about it.

We pasted on smiles and waved good-bye as the white van drove off, leaving puffs of dust.

"You pulled it out of the fire, Maggie," Jen said, patting her friend on the back.

"Yeah," I admitted. "Now all we have to do in five easy lessons is teach them how to ride, then turn them into performers."

12

On Tuesday, I didn't see anybody else at Horsefeathers, but I could tell somebody had ridden Bruiser while I wasn't there. I didn't talk with Maggie or Jen or Carla, although I was sure they would have talked to each other. I just hoped they'd all remember to show up for the second King's Kamp riding lesson.

B.C., Dotty, and I left the house at the same time Wednesday morning. A warm, fresh, minty smell met us on the front porch. "It didn't rain last night, did it?" I asked. Nothing looked wet—not the steps or the car or the grass.

"Well, it done thought about it," Dotty said, tugging on the warped screen door to get it to shut far enough to discourage flies from slipping in. "Right early this morning I heard pitter pats on the roof. By the time I got outside, the sprinkle was done. But it's brung in clean air and heaven smells, ain't it?"

B.C. and I walked Dotty to her car. "How come you're leaving so late?" he asked her.

Dotty yawned. "Them prayer requests folks

turned in Sunday ... " She yawned again. "I had to put them together for the prayer meeting tonight. Don't reckon I can make the meeting though. I told Mr. Ford I'd stay late to make up for coming in late."

Dotty reminded me of a ground hog burrowing into his hole as she wriggled herself behind the steering wheel. "You two have fun now!" she ordered, pulling the door shut. "Say hey to Carla and Maggie and Jen and everybody for me. I'm asking Mr. Ford for time off to see that there show you boys is putting on. Wild horses couldn't keep me away from that!" She laughed at her own horse joke.

B.C. chattered at me all the way to Horsefeathers, but I wasn't listening. I was going over my plans for our second King's Kamp riding lesson. I hoped Maggie and Jen hadn't tried to map out lessons on their own. One thing was for sure—we'd have to let the boys actually ride the horses this time. If we didn't, even Maggie wouldn't be able to put down the mutiny.

"Look!" B.C. shouted when we turned up Horsefeathers Lane. "Carla's riding!"

I couldn't believe it. Carla Buckingham had come early to work with Bruiser? I was glad she had. Bruiser hadn't been terrible on Monday, but he never did relax. Riding the feistiness out of him before the lesson might do him a world of good.

Carla was at the far end of the paddock. All I could make out was her head bobbing up and down. As we got closer, it was clear she was posting. And when we reached the paddock, I could see she wasn't riding Bruiser at all. She was working out English with her own horse, Buckingham's British Pride, posting up and down as if she were in an English equitation competition. A lot of good that would do keeping the horses out of the slaughterhouse.

B.C. waved at her and ran up to the fence to watch. She waved back, ignoring me completely. I set to work in the barn, graining the other horses and mucking out stalls.

Every now and then I walked out to the front of the barn and stared down the lane. But nobody came. It hadn't occurred to any of them that I could use some help before the lesson.

At 8:30, I started to worry that Travis would be late dropping Jen off and driving out to King's Kamp to pick up the boys and Ms. Mansfield.

At 9:15, I gave up on Jen and decided she must have gone with Travis to King's Kamp, instead of being dropped off at Horsefeathers first. I saddled Red and Babe and groomed them for lessons.

Carla cooled off Ham and turned him out to pasture. Without so much as a hello to me, she took Bruiser to the cross-ties and began brushing him. I heard him paw the ground in protest to being touched. Again, I wished she'd taken the extra time with Bruiser instead of her own horse. Didn't she know how much I ached to ride my own horse? Or didn't she care?

"Greetings!" Maggie 37 Green bounded into the barn just as I was saddling Dusty. She was sporting green jeans, green T-shirt, a green cowboy hat, and green boots that looked brand new.

I had Dusty in the cross-ties, already brushed. I'd even cleaned out his hooves in case Maggie arrived late. With the big Roan's saddle in my hands, I felt as if I'd been caught red-handed.

"Thanks for getting Dusty ready for me," Maggie said.

"You're welcome," I said, relieved she didn't think I was trying to take over *her* horse. I smoothed the saddle blanket and eased on the saddle.

"We'll be done at 11, right?" Maggie asked. She scratched Dusty under his jaw, and he closed his eyes.

"I guess," I said, squatting under his belly and pulling the cinch around from the other side.

"Good," Maggie said. "Because I have to run right at 11. Theater rehearsals."

Figures. I sighed and held my tongue. Maggie had a lifetime of rehearsals. We only had two weeks of lessons. I changed the subject. "Travis didn't drop Jen off like he did last time," I said. "I guess they were running late."

"No," Maggie said, getting Dusty's bridle from the hook by his stall. "Didn't you hear? Jen's not coming."

"She what?" The tightened saddle strap slid through my fingers before I could get it tied.

"Jen can't come today." Maggie said it matter-of-factly, as if it didn't matter.

"But—" I forced myself not to say what I was thinking. I knew Jen's reasons for not coming had to be better than Maggie's excuses, but it didn't help. It wouldn't make the lessons go any easier. "Did she have a doctor's appointment?"

"No," Maggie said, stretching on tiptoes of her green boots to put the earpiece over Dusty's ear. "Her nausea's back. You know, where she does that dry heave thing in the mornings, but nothing comes up?" She shuddered. "Jen says it's no big deal, but I'd sure hate to start my days like that. Mrs. Zucker's making Jen take it easy for a couple of days. Jen thinks she'll be fine by Friday's lesson."

I hadn't known about the "dry heave thing." I pictured Jen waking up and running to the toilet, holding back her blonde hair, and heaving. My stomach churned for her, and I prayed God would heal her kidneys. I wished Jen had called me.

A horn honked outside.

"They're early!" Maggie cried.

Carla had Bruiser saddled, but the Pinto didn't look happy about it. Neither did Carla. I hurried and slipped bridles on Babe and Red and reached the paddock as the boys were climbing the fence.

B.C. took up his cowardly position behind me as I led the two horses to the center of the arena. "Where's Jen?" he whispered. "I don't see Jen. She's supposed to help me with Babe. Where is she? I can't ride all by myself, Scoop. What are we going to do?"

"It's all right, B.C.," I said, trying to shake him loose from me.

Travis waved. "Hey, B.C.! Guess what. Guess who gets to be your partner today."

B.C. didn't guess.

"Me! How about that! That okay with you and Babe? I'm covering for Jen this morning. She says you hardly need help anyway."

B.C. came out of hiding and stroked Babe's neck. "Did Jen really say that?"

"Travis!" Maggie yelled, pulling hard on the giant Roan to get him out to the paddock. "Did you bring them?" She dropped Dusty's reins into Travis's palm. "Did you?"

"Yep," said Travis.

"Bring what?" I asked. I was feeling farther and farther out of the loop with every minute.

"Where are they?" Maggie asked, totally ignoring me.

"In the back of the van. They're in the cardboard box marked *Horsefeathers.*"

Maggie ran past me. I waited for Travis to fill me in, but he didn't. Instead, he called to his brother. "Tommy! Quit fighting and come get your horse."

Tommy ran up to Travis and Dusty. He stood right in front of the Blue Roan and stared up at him. "How old is this horse anyway? He looks like he's a thousand years old."

"I can show you how to tell his age by his teeth," I volunteered.

"Yuk! No way!" Tommy looked at me as if I'd just asked him to climb into Dusty's mouth and be swallowed so he could check out the horse's insides.

"Need any help?" Travis hollered to Maggie.

She waved him off, then hoisted a big cardboard box out of the van.

"Eric, Eric," Ms. Mansfield was saying, as she dragged him out of the barn toward us. "Tommy and David were just teasing you. I told you that in the van. Horses do not think red hair is good to eat. None of the horses will try to eat your hair."

Eric didn't look convinced.

"Step aside!" David yelled, shoving Tommy out of the way just to be sure his orders were obeyed. "The star of the show is coming through!" He seemed even thinner than on Monday. His eyes had deep circles under them, and his cheeks sank into his jaw. My first guess was that he'd stayed up all night.

Carla waved to David as if she were glad to see him. "Bruiser's been waiting for you," she said.

"Morning, Ms. Mansfield," I said.

She looked around, probably trying to find Maggie.

"Maggie!" I yelled. She was taking forever to get back with the big box. "We have to get started!" *Especially since Maggie is the one who has to leave early.*

"We better get to ride this time," David said. It sounded like a threat.

"Yeah!" Tommy agreed. "I'm riding really fast."

"I'm riding faster than you are!" David shouted.

"Are not!" Tommy shouted back.

"Am too!"

"Are not!"

"Am too!"

Ms. Mansfield broke up the shouting match. "Neither of you boys will ride at all without a helmet. Travis, where are those helmets I gave you last time?"

"I told you!" David yelled. "I'm not wearing that dumb helmet. I hate it! It smashes my hair!"

"I'm not wearing that dumb helmet either!" Tommy said. "They're stupid."

"Well then," said Ms. Mansfield, "we might as well turn right around and drive back to King's Kamp. Travis?"

Maggie, breathing hard, dropped the box at David's and Tommy's feet. "Pshew! Did I hear somebody say he's not wearing a hat? That's too bad," she said, opening the flaps and reaching into the box. She came out with a brown cowboy hat. "Because I don't understand how you can even be in a Wild West Show without a cowboy hat."

"Cool!" David exclaimed.

"Wow!" Tommy said, reaching for the hat. "I want it!"

David shoved Tommy away. "Give it to me! That's *my* hat!"

Maggie pulled out another hat just like the first one. Only then did I notice the rim of white sticking out from the brim. Ms. Mansfield's helmets were hidden inside the cowboy hats.

"Step right up, cowboys!" Maggie passed one hat to each of the boys and flashed a smile to Ms. Mansfield.

"Very nice," said Ms. Mansfield. "You keep those hats on at all times, boys."

"No sweat!" David said, smoothing his hair under his hat.

I watched as the boys adjusted their cowboy hats. Maggie 37 had done it again. She'd turned the hated helmets into cowboy hats the boys fought over. I should have thought of doing that myself, but I never would have in a million years.

13

The boys were so anxious to get riding that I couldn't even make it all the way through the little talk I'd prepared on joining up and on riding safety. I gave up, and in 10 minutes they were all standing by their horses, ready to mount and raring to go.

B.C. and Eric accepted the hay bales we pulled out as mounting blocks. Tommy and David shoved theirs away. But when Tommy realized how far up Dusty really was, and that he'd have to raise his foot neck-high to reach the stirrup, he finally let Maggie drag his bale back.

"I don't need any sissy cry baby mounting block!" David insisted. I wanted Carla to make him use one of the bales. But instead, she let him have his own way.

Before I could start instructing them, Maggie 37 was calling out the orders. "First, check your saddle girth. If it's not tight, you'll be riding upside down under your horse's belly!" She waited while they checked their saddles.

Eric was so scared, I tightened Red's saddle

a bit, even though it didn't need to be tightened. Travis let B.C. pull Babe's strap, which my brother loved. I glanced over at Bruiser. The minute David touched the big, silver saddle, Bruiser sidestepped.

"Face the tail," Maggie said. "Now, take the stirrup in your right hand and turn it toward you. Stick your *left* foot in the stirrup—unless you want to end up riding backwards! Okay now. When I say 'hi-ho!' I want you to take three little hops, then swing that right leg over—"

"Wait!" I shouted. "Don't grab the saddle horn! And don't try to hold on to the front and back of the saddle." I didn't know half of what Maggie and Carla knew about the proper way to mount a horse. Maggie knew I ride Orphan bareback. But I'd seen enough to sense what horses feel when riders throw them off balance with sloppy mounts.

"Just grab the pommel of your saddle!" I shouted.

But it was too late. David had his saddle gripped front and back, trying to pull himself up. Bruiser walked off, just to keep his balance. Carla had her hands full.

Even with the bale of hay, Tommy barely reached Dusty's stirrup. Maggie pushed him the rest of the way up. B.C. made it by himself, but I had to lift Eric onto Red's saddle. Still, somehow, every boy ended up on a horse.

We led horses and riders around the ring at a walk. Eric never let go of the saddle horn. Every two minutes, he told me, "I want off."

"Giddyup!" Tommy cried, as Dusty and Maggie fell farther behind. Maggie tried to get the Roan to walk faster, but nothing she did made a difference. "I hate this horse! Make him go!" Tommy shouted.

Bruiser's quick-paced walk propelled him past the other horses until Carla and Bruiser and David were right on Red's heels. "Scoop!" Carla called up to me. "Shouldn't we teach them a balanced seat?"

When I didn't answer fast enough, Carla took it upon herself to try to perfect the riders. "Boys!" she shouted. "Don't sit so far forward. Sit up straight. And move back. Legs straight down—not out in front of you. Toes up! Heels down!"

Maggie chimed in. "Keep the ball of your foot on the stirrup! Don't stick your foot in too far."

Every time we passed Ms. Mansfield, she felt it her duty to add her two cents and warn us: "Be careful! Don't fall off!"

I wasn't having a bit of fun. I was pretty sure the boys weren't either. And I knew the horses weren't enjoying themselves.

"Hold it, everybody!" I shouted. "Look. Just forget all the riding advice you're hearing.

Instead, pay attention to your horse. Relax! Join up with your horse and forget everything else."

Dusty had fallen so far behind, the rest of us almost lapped him. Red and I were coming up fast on his tail. Suddenly Maggie stopped. I had to pull up Red fast to avoid ramming into Dusty. Carla had to move Bruiser out of line. Babe and Travis and B.C. fell in behind Red.

"It's 11:00," Maggie said. "Time to quit. Off you go, Tommy!"

Maggie took off, leaving me to take care of Dusty, on top of everything else. Travis had to drive everybody back to King's Kamp, which meant I also got Babe to cool down and groom.

Carla took care of Bruiser. Before she left, she stopped by Red's stall. "I don't know what's wrong with Bruiser," she admitted. "I can't get him to settle down. He never did stop moving when David was on his back."

"I noticed," I said. "Do you mind if I work on him tomorrow?"

"Be my guest," she said. Then she turned and left me alone to finish grooming the horses, mucking the stalls, and picking up the pieces.

Thursday I took a quick morning ride on Orphan. Then I turned all my attention to Bruiser. It was the chance I'd been waiting for, to see if I could figure out what was going on with the Pinto.

Bruiser didn't like it when I brushed him.

And he flinched when I swung up on his back. But after a few times around the paddock arena, he relaxed.

I rode Bruiser bareback for a couple of hours—through the stream, around the pastures, back in the woods. He rode like a dream, enjoying the ride almost as much as I did. I wished Carla could have been there to see it. But she never showed up. She was more than likely out with Ray. How could I expect her to be bothered with Horsefeathers and the very real possibility that Bruiser and the King's horses could end up at the slaughterhouse?

~~~~~~~~~~~~~~~~~~~~~~~~~~~~

On Friday at our next practice, Maggie was the one who didn't show.

"She's got rehearsals or something," Jen said, as we saddled our horses. Travis had dropped Jen off early, and she had pitched right in, mucking as many stalls as I had.

"I can't believe Maggie didn't bother to call me," I complained.

"Travis said he'd keep an eye on Dusty and Tommy," Jen said. "It will all work out fine."

"Easy for you to say," I muttered. Maggie knew how important the lessons were. After this lesson, we'd only have three more chances to get ready for the show *she'd* gotten us into. Maggie had seen how upset I was when Jen didn't show up for Wednesday's lesson. And still, she didn't so much as lift a finger to call me.

Our riding lesson got off to a choppy start. Tommy and David arrived, already fighting mad at each other. Eric Rudd seemed more frightened than ever. Maggie wasn't there to smooth Ms. Mansfield's feathers. But 15 minutes into the lesson they were all on their horses, being led around the arena.

"Let go!" Tommy cried. "You're making this big ox go too slow!"

Dusty was in no hurry, and Travis didn't have any more luck speeding up the Roan than Maggie had. "Doing the best I can, Tommy," Travis said. "But here you go. Ride 'em, cowboy!"

Travis shocked Tommy *and* me by letting go of Dusty's reins. Then he turned his back on Tommy and Dusty and walked away. Tommy's hands flew to the saddle horn. His eyes widened. Dusty kept walking exactly as he had been.

Finally, Tommy relaxed and took the reins back into his left hand, without releasing the horn from his right hand. "That's better!" Tommy shouted. "Giddyup!"

"Let go of my horse too!" David cried. "I want to ride by myself!"

No, Carla. No. Don't let go. Don't listen to him.

Carla Buckingham did as she was told by Emperor David Miller and joined Travis in the center of the arena.

"What do you say, B.C.?" Jen asked.

I saw my brother glance at Tommy and David before he answered. "Yeah. Let go."

Jen joined Maggie and Travis in the center of the arena.

"Do *you* want me to let go of Red?" I asked Eric.

Eric shook his head so hard I was afraid he'd get dizzy and fall off. His arms stiffened, and I had a feeling Red's saddle horn would have fingernail marks on it.

Travis appeared behind me. "Move over, Scoop. Hi, Eric. Could I lead Red for a while? We can let Scoop here take a break." He winked at me and took Red's reins. The horse didn't miss a stride.

Jen and Carla were deep in conversation when I reached them. I watched our riders. B.C. and Tommy looked very serious. I couldn't read David's expression. His eyes had narrowed to slits, and frown lines covered his face as if he were in pain.

"Good idea," Carla was saying to Jen. "Go ahead." She nodded toward the horses and riders.

For the rest of that lesson, Jen was the instructor, calling out pointers that the boys ignored until finally Ms. Mansfield came over and collected them.

On Monday, all instructors showed up,

although Maggie was late and wasted no time putting us all on edge. I didn't bring up the fact that she'd left us in a lurch on Friday, and neither did she.

"Where's the other hat?" Maggie cried. She hadn't even thanked me for saddling Dusty for her. "We've only got three hats! How could you lose one?"

"Too bad you weren't here to count hats, Maggie," I said.

Travis drove up in the King's Kamp van. David was first to hop out. He was wearing the missing hat. Travis said David had it on when he picked him up, and he never took it off the whole time he was at Horsefeathers. "It's *my* hat, and you can't have it!" David insisted. And of course, Carla let him do what he wanted.

Mounting went pretty smoothly, and the boys started in riding where they'd left off. David led the way with Bruiser, who walked stiffer and stiffer. He'd lost all of the flexibility he'd shown on my bareback ride with him. The rest of us gravitated to the center of the arena.

Jen cleared her throat. "I want you to think about your position in the saddle," she began. "Eric, hold the reins in your left hand, and let that right hand relax down at your side, on your right thigh. Reins are too tight, David! B.C., sit deeper in the saddle! Tommy, you're tilting your rein shoulder! Keep your left hand in the middle.

Move it forward more!"

Horsefeathers! I was getting nervous just listening to her. After all, we were Horsefeathers Stable—not some fancy Western Horsemanship class. I wanted the boys to love horses, to bond with them, to *join up*. But Jen was making horsemanship seem like schoolwork.

"No, no, no!" Jen shouted. "I should be able to draw an imaginary line perpendicular to the horizon from your ear, to your shoulder, to the point of your hip, to the back of your heel."

That did it. "Listen up!" I shouted. "Forget all of that. Just listen to your horse. Ride! Have fun! Trust your horse. Learn to read him. Are his ears straight forward? Then he's worried about something ahead of him. Talk to him. Are his ears flat back? He's probably thinking about taking a bite out of that horse's rump in front of you. Keep your distance. Are his ears swiveling, one up and one back? He's doing fine. He's just paying you attention."

I felt Jen's glare, but I ignored her.

"Check out his tail," I continued. "If he's swinging it in circles, like Red there, he's anxious and not very happy. Talk to him, Eric. See how high Bruiser holds his tail? He's excited about something. Try to figure out what, David."

As I talked, Jen moved back to Babe's side. I saw her whisper something to B.C. Maggie, too, left me for Dusty and Tommy. Carla had left, but

I spotted her at the paddock fence, talking to Ray. I didn't know when he'd shown up.

I stood there, alone in the center of the arena, getting angrier and angrier. Two more lessons, and these boys were going to put on a show? "Canter!" I yelled, before I'd made the conscious decision to speed things up.

"Yippee!" Tommy cried. "Go!" He tried to push Dusty into a canter. Dusty jogged, then trotted, taking his time getting there.

Red responded immediately, breaking into a gentle lope. Eric screamed and grabbed the saddle horn, while Travis ran to keep up. Babe followed suit and cantered. B.C. grabbed the horn, his eyes wide as full moons.

In the front, Bruiser leaped into a canter that made David squeal. "Yeehaw!" David shouted. Bruiser took that to mean *Go faster!* He moved into a gallop that quickly brought him all the way around the ring, closing the distance on Red, who held a steady canter.

"Carla!" I screamed.

Carla was already running toward Bruiser. But the gap between the Pinto and Red was getting shorter and shorter. "Pull back, David!" she yelled, running behind him, her arms flailing.

Bruiser took *that* to mean *Go faster!* too. He surged ahead, ramming into Red's rump. Red's legs slid in the dust as he ground to a halt. Eric let out a spine-chilling scream that brought Ms.

Mansfield to the rescue.

Carla grabbed Bruiser's reins and pulled him to a walk. David looked like he might be sick. Travis and Jen had Babe under control, but B.C. was crying. Tommy Zucker was cheering because Dusty had finally gone faster.

Ms. Mansfield was screaming at all of us. "What made me think that you *children* could train horses *or* boys for King's Kamp? I will be calling Ralph Dalton about these *creatures!*"

My heart pounded from anger and fear. Eric was screaming, "Get me off! Get me off!" I lifted him down, and he ran to the van. Red balked and wouldn't let me lead him away.

Carla walked up with David and Bruiser. David still looked pale. He hadn't spoken.

"Why did you have to go so fast, David?" I cried, tears pressing behind my eyes. "And you, Carla? Why couldn't you stay with David instead of running off to Ray? I should have known better than to leave Bruiser to you!"

Carla's face turned red and splotchy. She fixed on me with a stare so cold I felt it in my boots. "Fine," she said, dropping Bruiser's reins. "I quit!"

14

With Carla gone, I had to get to Horse-feathers at dawn on Wednesday. Two more lessons. That's all we had left, and I had to beg Ms. Mansfield to get them. Tuesday she phoned to say she would be bringing the King's Kamp Board of Directors to the show on Saturday. That way they could evaluate for themselves whether or not the horses would be a good addition to King's Kamp.

I had the horses grained and the grooming half done when Travis dropped off Jen at Horse-feathers. She didn't have much to say, but she did take care of getting Babe ready.

I'd moved on to Bruiser and had him in the cross-ties when Maggie ran in, out of breath. "Am I late?"

She was. She stopped in the stallway and watched me try to brush the antsy Bruiser. "I still can't believe Carla really quit! I thought she'd show up today as if nothing had happened."

"I don't think I'd hold my breath on that one," Jen said. It made me think she and Carla had been talking behind my back.

"But how can she quit—with the show on Saturday and all? Bruiser needs more attention than the others." Maggie still made no move to get Dusty ready. "What are we supposed to do about Bruiser?"

"It's not a problem," I said. "We don't need Carla."

"But what about Bruiser?" Maggie asked. "*He* needs Carla."

I stopped brushing and turned to Maggie. "I'd rather handle Bruiser myself. That's the way it was supposed to work out in the first place. Bruiser will be better off without Carla."

Bruiser chose that moment to jerk his head up and pull against the cross ties. He pawed the ground.

"He does not look better to me," Jen said.

For once, I was relieved to see the white van drive up. I let Travis handle Red, and I took over with Bruiser and David. David didn't even slow down when he hit the paddock. He ran right up to Bruiser and stuck his foot in the stirrup. Before I could object, he'd pulled himself up in an off-balance mount that could have toppled poor Bruiser.

Tommy and B.C. managed to get on their horses. But not Eric Rudd. Eric sat cross-legged in the middle of the arena and folded his arms. "I'm not riding!" he screamed.

Travis tried everything he could to get Eric to give Red a chance. He even promised him ice cream. But Eric refused to budge. So did Red. He balked when Travis tried to lead him to the barn. Travis finally ended up getting the horse to the center of the arena and leaving Eric and Red right where they were.

Twenty minutes into the lesson, Maggie disappeared. When she reappeared, she was riding Moby, her own white mare. "Everybody line up in the middle here!" Maggie shouted. "We have to work on our show." Maggie leaned forward, and Moby bowed low in a graceful welcome.

"Cool!" Tommy shouted. "I want my horse to do that!"

Dusty would never bow like that, and Maggie should have known better than to plant the idea in Tommy's head. But the big Roan followed the others into the center of the arena. Jen and Travis led the horses into a straight line with Red, who still hadn't moved. Eric hadn't moved either, but he turned his head to watch.

Maggie showed off for the boys by having Moby paw the ground, counting to 24, her age. "We don't have time to teach your horses to count," Maggie admitted. "Besides, we don't even know how old they are. But I'll bet you can make your horse back up."

It was something I'd taught them the third lesson, the one Maggie had missed.

"We can already do that!" Tommy said, tugging on Dusty's reins until the Roan took one step backward.

Babe and Bruiser backed too. Bruiser kept backing up so fast I had to grab his reins and bring him up to the line again. "We already covered backing, Maggie," I said. "You would have known that if you'd been here for all the lessons."

"Okay then ..." Maggie hesitated, as if figuring out where to go from there. "I know! We'll start by rehearsing the *end* of the show. My drama coach always makes me start at the finish. A show is nothing without a strong finish."

Maggie put one hand on her yellow cowboy hat that matched her yellow jeans and shirt. "Now here's something all of you can do!" she exclaimed. "Even you, Eric. Grab the brim of your hat in your right hand."

The boys looked suspicious, but eventually, all right hands went to hat brims.

"When I say 'Yippee!,' I want you to toss your hats as high into the air as you can. Ready? 'Yippee!' " Maggie frisbee-tossed her yellow hat.

"Mine's going the farthest!" Tommy shouted. He threw his hat so hard, Travis had to duck.

B.C. glanced at me, then tossed his hat a few feet in front of Babe. It landed with a clunk and spun in the dirt.

"Go on, Eric!" Maggie coaxed.

Eric frowned. Then he picked up his helmet hat and threw it overhand, making it bounce once in the dirt.

"Great!" Maggie cried. "Now you, David!"

David, with one hand still on the brim, frowned at Maggie. "No."

"What?" Maggie asked. "You *have* to toss your hat toward the crowd," Maggie explained. "That's what happens in every Wild West Show. You'll get the hat back."

David removed his hand from the brim, and slammed his palm on top of the hat. "I'm not taking it off."

Maggie tried to change his mind, but he didn't give in. "Well," she said, looking deflated, "I guess that's not something you'll need to practice—as long as you do it on Saturday for the show."

David didn't say anything, and Maggie changed gears. "Now, I think it would be nice to start the show with a figure 8 ride."

"What's that?" B.C. asked, sounding like he didn't think he could do it.

"Moby and I will show you," Maggie said. "I'll ride my horse around you in a figure 8. Then you can try it."

My stomach felt like galloping horses were parading through it. All of this was a waste of time. What did parents care about riding in a figure 8? What did the King's Kamp board members care about tossing hats? What we needed was to work with boys and horses on the ordinary parts of riding. I knew the boys were still miles away from bonding with their horses. Horses and boys were all living in their separate little worlds, without any sense of joining up.

Maggie 37 Yellow raced Moby into the arena.

"I want to go fast like that!" Tommy yelled.

"I can do that!" David shouted.

Maggie slowed Moby to a lope and started her figure 8 where Jen was standing. She looped past me, circled Tommy and Bruiser, crossed between Eric and David, did the bottom loop, and headed back around.

As Maggie closed her imaginary figure 8, Moby brushed against Bruiser. Bruiser took one step and bumped Red. Red skidded back in fear and bashed into Babe. B.C. screamed. Bruiser picked up on the fear and jerked loose. David yelled, "Hey!"

Suddenly Bruiser bolted from the pack and ran toward the barn. "Duck! Duck, David!" I shouted. Bruiser cantered straight at the barn just as Ms. Mansfield was coming out.

"Help!" she cried. Ms. Mansfield jumped out of the way, falling into the dirt, as Bruiser sped past her and into his stall. There he stopped.

I ran to David and Bruiser, while Travis and

Jen saw to Ms. Mansfield. "You okay, David?" I asked. His cheeks were so sunken, that in the shadow of the stall, his head looked like a skull under his cowboy hat.

"Let me sit here a minute." David didn't sound scared. He didn't sound mad. He sounded tired.

I let him sit still while I checked Bruiser over. The Pinto wasn't scared, but his back twitched, as if he had a fly he was trying to get rid of.

"David!" Ms. Mansfield's cry reached us in the barn. "We're leaving!"

I helped David down, and he walked out of the barn to the van, his head down. I went back to Ms. Mansfield, who was still brushing paddock dust off of her tan slacks. "David's okay," I said. "Are you all right?"

"Quite frankly," she said stiffly, "I am not. This is exactly the kind of problem I was afraid of with these horses. I'll let the boys come back for the final lesson. But unless I see a great deal of improvement in the horses and the riders, I see no way we can allow these ... these ... creatures onto King's Kamp grounds."

Jen took Babe into the barn, and B.C. ran to the loft. Maggie and I watched Travis drive away with the King's Kamp crew. My nightmare flashed back to my mind, the line of horses drawing closer to the slaughterhouse.

"I wonder what got into Bruiser," Maggie said.

I turned to stare at her. Was it possible she was so out of touch she didn't see what she'd done? "*You*, Maggie," I shouted. "*You* are what got into Bruiser! You and your little show-off show."

"Me?" Maggie shouted back.

"I don't know why you bother coming here, Maggie! You have your head in theater rehearsals!"

Jen jogged out of the barn toward us. "Hey, you two! What's the shouting about?"

"Ask Scoop!" Maggie said. "*She's* the one who knows everything."

"I know enough not to start a horse stampede just because I want to show off—"

"Fine!" Maggie cried. "And you know what? Carla was right. I quit too!"

Moby reared and pivoted, and Maggie rode off at a gallop.

"Scoop," Jen said, "you didn't mean that. You should go after her. Apologize."

"*Me?*" I couldn't believe Jen wanted *me* to apologize. Maggie was the one who hadn't pulled her weight the whole time we'd had lessons. *She* was the one who made Bruiser bolt. Because of her, Ms. Mansfield could send the horses to the slaughterhouse. And nobody seemed to care except me. "No way!" I said. "You're the ones who should be apologizing."

"Me?" Jen cried. "What did *I* do?"

"Not enough." The words were out before I could stop them.

Jen straightened her wire-rimmed glasses and stepped back as if I'd struck her. "Have it your way then." She turned and walked away.

"Jen! I'm sorry. I didn't mean it."

Jen didn't slow down or turn around. She ran to catch Maggie.

Fine! Let them leave. Let them all leave! Carla can have Ray. Jen and Maggie can have each other. I don't need any of them!

15

I couldn't sleep that night. I was afraid I'd have my nightmare. When I tried to pray, I'd end up making mental lists of everything I had to do before Saturday. Visions of Ms. Mansfield and King's Kamp board members (all of them looking like a version of Ms. Mansfield) trudged through my head.

Stars filled the sky and lit my attic room with cast-off light. I stayed in bed as long as I could, but it was no use. I kicked off my sheet and lay sweating until I couldn't take it anymore.

Finally I pulled on jeans and a T-shirt and headed downstairs. I'd need an early start anyway. I'd have to exercise all the horses on my own. In my mind, I ran over the riding exercises I'd put the boys through on Friday.

The hallway was pitch black. I groped for the banister and felt for the top stair with my toes. Taking another step, I sensed the stairs underfoot. My bare foot came down on something cold and sharp. I tried to step away, but my other foot slipped. Both feet slid out from under me. My shoulder hit the railing, bouncing me backward. I landed on the side of my foot. My ankle crumpled and sent me crashing down the stairs, rolling, thumping down, down, down. Sparks went off behind my eyeballs.

I heard myself hit the bottom landing with a thump. For a second I felt nothing. The only sound was my rasping breath. A door banged somewhere. I heard footsteps. A light went on.

"Dear Jesus, help her!" Dotty cried. "Are you hurt? What happened?" She knelt beside me. "Scoop, speak to me!"

"I'm okay," I said, trying to straighten my leg. "Ow!" My right foot throbbed. When I moved it, sharp pains shot up my shin. "My foot ..."

"Don't you go moving a muscle," Dotty said. "You hear?"

I glanced to the top of the stairs. There stood B.C., storm still. He leaned down and picked up the bottle caps, the ones I'd slipped on. "Is she going to die?" he asked softly.

"Good gracious, no!" Dotty declared. "Come on down here and see for yourself!"

My anger at B.C. for leaving his bottle caps out where I could trip over them was already melting into fear for him. "I just tripped, B.C.," I said, grunting after every word. Pain had climbed down to my toes and up as far as my knee.

B.C. sat down on the top stair. He threw the

bottle caps over the banister into the living room. They clattered like coins. Then he wrapped his arms around his knees and rocked.

"You reckon we can get you to the car?" Dotty asked, examining my foot, which was blowing up like a football. "Or you reckon I oughta call us an ambulance?"

"No, Dotty!" I cried. "I have to get to Horsefeathers!" I leaned forward and took hold of the railing to pull myself up. "Yeow!" It felt like pins were sticking into my foot.

Dotty helped me stand up. Every other part of my body seemed to be unbroken. One elbow had a king-sized splinter, and my back ached. But as long as I kept my weight off my right foot and leaned on Dotty, I was okay.

Dotty drove B.C. and me to the hospital and ran inside the emergency glass doors. B.C. wouldn't speak to me the whole time we sat in the car waiting for her. "It's not your fault," I told him. "I wasn't looking where I was going."

He stared out the window when a white ambulance drove up beside us. The driver got out and walked inside. I wondered if he'd had a false alarm and come back empty-handed.

Two men in green hospital shirts rolled out a stretcher for me. Despite my protests, they made me ride in on it. I watched the stars change to green plaster ceiling as they rolled me inside and down the hall.

A doctor saw us right away. He smiled with his mouth, but his eyes squinted the whole time he examined me. I guessed he was the age my dad would have been. And like I do every time something bad happens, I wondered if I would have fallen down the stairs if my dad had still been alive.

The doctor sent us to the basement for X-rays. I had to ride in a wheelchair pushed by a nurse who was smaller than me. They took pictures of my foot, turning it and posing it until I thought I'd cry. They X-rayed my shin, my knee, and my hip.

We waited on straight-backed chrome chairs outside the X-ray room. It smelled like alcohol. Dotty had made friends with the people on either side of us—a white-haired woman who had fallen in her kitchen, and a little girl in a cast. If the girl had been a horse, she'd have been an ornery Shetland—broken leg or not. She'd been working hard to get my brother's attention, but for all I knew, B.C. didn't know she was there. His eyes had a glazed-over look.

Finally, the doctor came out. "Well, Miss Coop. You are one lucky lady. Not a single broken bone."

"Thank You!" Dotty exclaimed. "And thank you too, Doc!"

"Congratulations!" said the old woman. "Not broken."

"*My* leg was broken for real!" the girl said. "I wasn't faking at all."

"Why does it hurt so much then?" I asked. I was glad my foot wasn't broken. But I didn't want anybody to think I was faking it.

"You didn't break bones, but you did sprain your ankle," the doctor explained. He reminded me of a Quarter Horse, somebody you could count on. "And you've torn several ligaments. I've wrapped it to help keep the swelling down. The nurse will come out and give you some crutches for—"

"Crutches? You're kidding, right?" It wasn't possible. I had riding lessons to give, a show to put on. "I can't use crutches."

The doctor grinned. "I'm afraid you'll have to get used to them. I don't want you to put any weight on that foot for at least 10 days. Come back and see me in—"

"But I can't!" My throat burned. I couldn't hold back tears.

"There, there," Dotty said, putting her arm around me. "Them 10 days will go by so fast you won't know what happened to them."

"You don't understand! I have to give lessons tomorrow. And put on a show Saturday!"

I glanced at B.C. He was staring at the doctor.

The nurse walked up with the crutches that were about as tall as she was. "And these must be for you," she said. "See how smart they make nurses here?" She pushed the crutches to me, but I wouldn't take them.

"Thank you kindly," Dotty said, taking the crutches for me.

The sun was up and hot as ever as Dotty drove us home. I rolled the window down as far as it would go. My upper arm hurt already just from using the stupid crutches out to the car.

"Drop me off at Horsefeathers, Dotty," I said as we drove past the Hy-Klas.

"Scoop," she said. "Hadn't you oughta rest that there foot like the doc says?"

"I will, Dotty," I said. "But I have to do chores."

"Scoop, you know right well Jen or Maggie or Carla would help out if we asked."

"No, Dotty," I said. "I'll do it myself. I don't need them to help."

"I'll feed the horses," B.C. whispered from the backseat.

"Thanks, B.C.," I said. "But I'm okay."

Dotty glanced over at me and sighed. But she turned the Chevy toward Horsefeathers. When we got there, she shut off the ignition, and I knew I was about to get a lecture.

"Did you ever wonder why God made Himself so many different kinds of horses?" Dotty stared at the pasture. Misty and Orphan had crossed the paddock to the near fence. Deep in the pasture, we could see the Palomino, the

Pinto, the big Blue Roan, and the Chestnut, besides the regular Horsefeathers horses.

I had my hand on the door latch, but I sat still.

"I reckon it's like with God's people. Sure would be boring if we was all to look alike. But I reckon it ain't just that. God's made Hisself a body of folks—some like fingers and toes, others like heads or ankles—each one fit for a different work. Ain't a one of them parts can make things work out by itself."

I opened the door a crack.

Dotty turned to B.C. in the backseat. "Can you just imagine what you'd look like with just toes?" She laughed. "Or just heads or hearts? I reckon I'm just about a toenail when it comes to keeping our church running. Lord knows them pews would soon come up empty if they was to put me at the organ!"

Even I grinned imagining Dotty playing the hymns. I glanced at B.C., and he grinned too.

"But I know the Lord, He needs them bulletins B.C. and me fold. And I don't reckon them missionaries could get them baskets without I done got that stuff they made it out of. I'd be feeling mighty left out and useless if nobody let me do what I can do—even if it ain't but a toe-full."

I knew what Dotty was getting at in her own way. Ms. Mansfield would have been giving her teamwork lecture. Dotty talked about toes. And I knew she was right. I've always liked it best when I could do everything by myself—just me and the horses. I hadn't thought about other people needing to help.

B.C. was staring at me with a hope I hadn't seen in him since I'd tripped on his bottle caps.

"Thanks, B.C.," I said, shutting the car door. "I'd appreciate the help." I gave him specific instructions, even though he'd watched me grain the horses a million times.

B.C. flew out of the car like a man on a mission. Dotty smiled like a woman who'd just successfully completed *her* mission.

"Okay, Dotty," I said, as we watched B.C. disappear into the barn. "You won this round. But you still have to promise that you won't call Maggie or Jen or Carla."

Dotty and I waited while B.C. fed and watered the horses. When he was finished, B.C. hopped back in the car with a satisfied look on his face that told me I'd done the right thing.

As she drove home, Dotty sang "What a Friend We Have in Jesus," and I thought about what she had said, that we're all part of the same body. Pastor Dan had said the same thing a couple of weeks ago, that God makes us all part of the body of Christ. I was glad Dotty reminded me of that. But when she got to the part of the song about our friends forsaking us, I couldn't help thinking that except for Dotty and B.C., Jesus was the only friend I had left in the world.

~~~~~~~~~~~~~~~~~~~~~~~~~~~~~~~

The rest of day I drifted in and out of sleep. The doctor had given me pills that made me feel like I was underwater and everybody else was up top. I remember B.C. standing over me and reporting about which horse did what at Horse-feathers. I remember Dotty beside the bed, begging me to let her call one of my "girlfriends" and tell them what happened. But even in my groggy condition, I was clear-headed enough to remind her of her promise not to call them.

Dotty made me come down for supper. I picked at the orange clumps in our Hy-Klas Macaroni and Cheez. The comma-shaped pasta may have been macaroni, but the dry stuff from the packet was definitely not cheese.

"I don't know what I'm going to do tomorrow, Dotty," I said. "It's our last practice, and the boys haven't joined up with their horses or with each other."

"It's David's fault," B.C. muttered. He'd skipped the macaroni and gone straight for his cup of chocolate pudding.

"I reckon you and Jesus will have to have you a heart-to-heart about this joining up," Dotty suggested. "And you might want to talk a spell about toes."

~~~~~~~~~~~~~~~~~~~~~~~~~~~~~

Friday morning it took me twice as long as normal to get dressed. None of my shoes or boots fit over the bandage, so I settled for one boot and one bare foot in Ace bandages. Exhausted, sweating from the heat already, I sat on the edge of my bed. My toes stuck out of the bandage, and I smiled remembering Dotty's *toe-talk*.

Lord, I prayed, *I have to admit that this King's Kamp show, even the lesson today, that's something I can't do by myself. I need You to help me*. The prayer didn't feel done. It's the same feeling I get when I've had a good ride on Orphan, but I sense there's more to it, that it's not time to stop yet.

Help me get the boys to join up with their horses and with each other. And teach me about toes today. Amen.

D otty dropped me off at Horsefeathers two
hours early for the final King's Kamp lesson. I knew that if I couldn't handle the riders by
myself, Ms. Mansfield would call the whole thing
quits. We wouldn't have a Saturday show to
worry about. And I didn't want to think about
where the horses would end up.

"You should of brung B.C.," Dotty said as
she pulled my crutches out of the back seat and
tried to help me out of the car.

Orphan and Misty came trotting up to the
paddock fence. Orphan nickered, then whinnied.

"I'm okay, Girl!" I shouted to her. "See,
Dotty?" I said, scooching both crutches under
my arm pits and hopping back from the car.
"Orphan will look out for me. Besides, B.C.
needs his sleep. Just make sure he gets up before
you leave for work."

"Don't ya think your friends would want to
know about your foot, Scoop? Let me call Maggie and—"

"You promised, Dotty," I said. I wanted

Maggie and Jen, and even Carla, more than Dotty did. Sure, I could have used their help with the horses and boys and Horsefeathers. But mostly, I missed them. And it hurt knowing that they wouldn't be missing me.

"Maggie and Jen and Carla don't want to help with this, Dotty," I said. "They've got other things to do. And I sure don't want them to show up just because they feel sorry for me."

Dotty's car was out of sight by the time I made it over to Orphan. She rubbed her beautiful head against my cheek. Misty tried to poke his nose between the fence boards to chew on my crutches.

"Can't you have a word with the horses, Orphan?" I scratched under her jaw. "Tell them to join up the way you and I have."

I left Orphan and Misty and hobbled into the barn to take care of morning feed. I hadn't counted on how hard it would be to carry the grain and move on crutches at the same time. Oats flew out of the measuring can every time I swung myself forward.

By the time I'd filled the feed troughs, the horses were neighing angrily at me for taking so long. Since there wasn't enough time to feed the herd in two shifts, I'd have to let them all in at once and then hope—and pray—for the best. The ground was so dry and hard in the paddock, it was like walking on cement. Every time I thrust my good foot forward, my bad foot hurt.

As I unlatched the pasture fences, Bruiser and Cheyenne battled for front position. Babe and Red must have been hungry because they tried to stand their ground. I eased the gate back a crack. Dusty walked straight up through the horses as if they weren't there. When he got to the gate, he kept walking.

I hopped back one step to open the gate wider, but I wasn't fast enough. Bruiser shoved Dusty, who stumbled into Angel and Moby, who bumped Cheyenne and Babe. I hopped back another step. One of my crutches slipped out of my sweaty hand. It fell to the dirt in slow motion, landing in front of Red.

Red reared, setting off the herd. Through the gate they charged, like mustangs in a stampede. Instead of heading for the barn, they kept trying to outrun each other. They squealed, bucking and kicking across the paddock. I stood helplessly while the horses tore around me, scaring up dust into a brown fog that made me cough.

Cheyenne landed a kick on Bruiser. The Pinto took his revenge out on Babe, then ran toward me, skidding to change directions just before he trampled me.

My eyes watered so I could hardly see. "Stop! Whoa!" I cried.

They didn't listen. Horses swirled around

me. Hooves appeared in clouds of dust as if the sky had finally fallen, bringing with it horses' hooves. Dust made my eyes clamp shut. I couldn't see Orphan beside me, but I could smell her.

"Scoop!" A hand clasped my arm. Then I felt myself being hoisted in a fireman-carry over somebody's shoulder.

I clung to the remaining crutch as I was carried several yards and set down next to the barn.

"Are you okay?" It was Travis. I'd never been more thankful to see him.

All I could muster was a nod. Dirt coated my mouth. I wiped my lips with the back of my hand and blinked to clean the dust out of my eyes.

"What should we do?" Ray yelled from the barn.

Travis and Ray rounded up the horses by stretching out their arms and walking the herd toward the barn. Somehow Travis got Bruiser inside. Then the others wound down and followed the Pinto to their stalls.

Travis ran over to me. "Are you hurt? Should I drive you to the hospital? They didn't step on your sprained ankle, did they?"

Dotty! I'd thought my aunt was the one person in the world I could count on to keep her word. "Dotty promised she wouldn't call."

"Easy, Scoop," Travis said, handing me the other crutch. It looked as if it had been stepped on, bent, but not broken. "Dotty said she promised not to call Jen. She didn't call Jen. She called me."

I should have known Dotty wouldn't break a promise. "I'm sorry, Travis. Thanks. Thanks for coming."

Ray stood a few feet away, just inside the barn. He shook his head and scratched his thick, black hair. "Horses," he muttered.

"What I don't get," Travis said, "is why *you* didn't call Jen. Or Maggie or Carla? Or me? None of us had any idea you were hurt."

"I didn't want you to know," I said, my throat burning from the mix of tears and dirt. "They quit, Travis. Horsefeathers isn't important to them—not like it is to me. I don't need their pity."

"You've got company!" Ray shouted.

For a split-second, I thought the King's Kamp boys had come early. Instead, Maggie and Jen were jogging toward us. They climbed the paddock fence and stared at me like I was a five-legged pony. Then they jogged across the paddock, silent and frowning.

"What happened?" Maggie asked. "Scoop, why are you on crutches?"

I couldn't talk. I couldn't do anything except sniff and sob in gasps.

"Scoop sprained her foot yesterday," Travis explained.

"And you didn't call us?" Jen asked.

Maggie burst into tears. "Why couldn't you call me? You make me so mad, Scoop!"

"Me?" I yelled. "You quit! Remember? You have more important things to bother about than Horsefeathers."

"More important things?" Maggie repeated. "Did it ever occur to you that maybe *I* wanted to be important to Horsefeathers?"

"What?" I snapped my mouth shut. Maggie's question stopped me cold. I was used to Maggie's excuses, Maggie's millions of things to do. But no. It had never occurred to me that Maggie wanted to be important to Horsefeathers. "I don't know what you're talking about, Maggie."

"You're the horse whisperer, Scoop," Maggie said. "You know how to get through to horses like nobody else in the world. I can't do that. *You're* the horse gentler. It's ... it's like this huge gift. Jen and I are good with horses, but not like you."

Jen nodded, agreeing with Maggie.

"But that doesn't mean we can't do anything—things that count!" Maggie caught a tear as it slid down her cheek. "Little things that count."

"I know that," I said, remembering all the times they'd left *everything* for me to do. "All month I needed help!" I said, swallowing dusty tears. "Where were *you* when I had to leave B.C. when he needed me just so I could do the chores?"

"We were a phone call away," Jen said softly. "And the last thing we would have imagined was that Sarah Coop needed anybody or anything."

The colt nickered behind us. A woodpecker beat regular rhythms from somewhere. I could almost hear Dotty whispering, *fingers, toes, ankles.*

"It's just ..." How could I explain it to them when I didn't understand it myself? "Well, it feels like if I don't do things myself, how can I know they'll get done? But I know I can't do it all on my own," I added quickly.

"Do you?" Maggie pointed to the barn. "Because it feels like you don't need us at all. And that's a rotten feeling."

I didn't know what to say. I couldn't imagine Maggie feeling unimportant anywhere. My mind flashed to Dotty and her bulletins, Dotty and her errands, Dotty and all the little things she does. She'd said those responsibilities made her feel an important part of the church.

"Look," Maggie said, no longer shouting, "I know I don't help out as much as I should at Horsefeathers, and I'm sorry, Scoop. I'm late most of the time. And I let you do way too much of the work. But it doesn't seem to matter if I'm here or not. Horsefeathers gets along fine when

I'm not here. It's hard to feel too bad about being gone. And when I *am* here, I can't seem to do anything right—not in your eyes anyway."

"That's not fair, Maggie," I said. "I never said—"

"You don't have to say it, Scoop. I feel it," Maggie said. "*Not* saying anything is enough sometimes. When I cleaned the stalls a couple of times during the week and you didn't say anything, I just figured you didn't like the way I did it. And you probably didn't like the way I soaped the saddles."

"*You* soaped the saddles?" I said, interrupting. "I thought the saddle shop cleaned them when Jen and Travis had the straps fixed. Maggie, I didn't know."

"We both worked on the saddles," Jen said. "That's why Maggie ended up spending the night at our house."

Why hadn't I just asked them? Why hadn't I trusted our friendship? "The saddles look terrific, you guys!" I said. "How could you think I didn't like them?"

"The same way you liked every plan I made for the show?" Maggie asked.

"That's different," I said. But it wasn't. I hadn't liked any of Maggie's ideas.

"Scoop," Jen said. "Come on. You hated it when I tried to give the boys riding tips. You didn't even approve of the way I cleaned out

Babe's hooves. I know you can't count on me to be here every day." She looked away.

I felt awful. "Oh, Jen ..." All the steam had leaked out of my defenses, and I had nothing left to say—no more excuses.

"We finally decided you didn't need us and would do better without us," Maggie said.

I could see it now. I'd made Maggie and Jen feel like toes I could get along without. *Lord, help me admit I need them.* Horses have to choose to join up, choose to work as a team. *Help me join up with my friends.*

"I'm so sorry," I said. "Please forgive me. I *do* need you. I couldn't do anything without you guys." And maybe for the first time, I understood how true those words were.

I took two sliding crutch-steps toward them before they raced to my rescue. "We're sorry too," Maggie said. "We should have said something before now." We fell into a hug, all three of us crying as loud as ... as a stampede.

"Women," Ray muttered.

I glanced at Travis. His eyes were watery. "Dust in my eyes," he said. I didn't believe him.

"What about Carla?" I asked. I turned to Ray. "Is that why she's been so mad at me? Did I make her feel like Horsefeathers didn't need her either?"

"Ask her yourself." Ray lowered his hand to his side and nodded toward the barn. I'd noticed his hands moving earlier, but I thought he was brushing away paddock dust. Instead, he'd been using sign language to relay to Carla everything we'd said.

Carla Buckingham stepped out from the barn shadows, her face streaked with tears. Maggie pulled her into our hug.

"I'm sorry," I said. "Forgive me?"

Carla didn't answer.

"Please, Carla," I said much louder.

She still didn't answer. Her head was buried in Maggie's shoulder. I felt the anger creep back in. Carla had plenty to apologize for too. It wasn't right for her not to say anything when I'd taken the first step toward making up. "Carla!" I screamed.

Jen and Maggie stared at me, then at Carla. I took a step back from our huddle and gazed at her. Finally, Carla raised her head. Her brow wrinkled as she glanced from one of us to the other.

"You didn't hear Scoop, did you, Carla?" Jen said gently.

I watched the way Carla's entire attention focused on Jen's lips. Why hadn't I seen it before? Carla dropped her head and shook it slowly.

Ray came up and stood across from Carla. "Tell them," he coaxed.

Carla sucked on her lips until I couldn't see

them. Finally she said, "I lost my hearing—all of it. I'm totally deaf."

"Carla, I didn't know!" I cried.

"It happened while Mother and I were in Spain. I've always known it could happen. But I never thought it would. To be honest, I didn't think it would be that big a deal. I didn't hear that great, even with my hearing aids. But it *is* a big deal."

She squinted up at Ray and then turned back to us. "I can't hear horses' hooves or Ham's whinny when I meet him in the pasture. I miss voices. But even more, I miss the little noises people make. The *hmmm's* and *ah's* and *mmm's* that keep people connected and let you know you're being listened to—that you're part of things."

I couldn't imagine what it would be like to lose the sound of Orphan's nicker, or her hooves in a dead-on gallop. "I didn't even suspect, Carla," I said. "Each time you didn't answer me, I thought you were ignoring me."

My mind paged back to the beginning, when I'd asked Carla to saddle Bruiser Western, and she'd come out with English gear. She hadn't heard me. And I'd thought she was mocking me, blowing me off on purpose. Had she even heard me when I asked her over the phone to meet me at Horsefeathers to ride?

"Why didn't you tell us?" I heard myself asking Carla the same thing Travis had asked me.

"I was afraid, Scoop. I knew you didn't think I could handle Bruiser."

"But—" I started to deny it, then stopped. Carla was right. I'd thought I was the only one who could handle that horse. How could I have gotten things so wrong? I'd been giving B.C. lectures on teamwork, when all the time *I* was the one who couldn't work as a team. I sent up a quick prayer, asking God to forgive me for my stubbornness and the careless way I had treated my friends. I finished my prayer, knowing God forgave me because of Jesus.

"I'm sorry, Carla. Will you forgive me?" I said, this time with her gaze on my lips. "I'd like to officially let it be known that I need all the help I can get."

"No kidding!" Maggie said, tapping my crutches. "Big news flash, Klutz."

It was the crack we needed to slide through, to get us from the pain to the laughter. We laughed so hard that joy tears sprang out of the sad tears.

Carla gave me a hug, and I knew that we were all okay again—a team.

Travis and Ray stood together, whispering.

"Travis!" I shouted. "What about the boys? Shouldn't you be at King's Kamp picking them up?"

"Not today," he answered. "Ms. Mansfield said she'd drive them in herself."

"So what are you girls standing around for?" I asked.

They grinned. "What do you need, Scoop?" Maggie asked.

Part of me wanted to seize control again and make sure the last lesson went exactly like I wanted it to. *Lord, help me trust.*

"What I really need," I said, glancing around at the horses, "... is a chair like Ms. Mansfield's. I think I'll be sitting this one out."

17

"O ne chair coming up!" Jen shouted, springing into action.

B.C. stuck his head out from the barn. "Is all the crying over?" he asked.

"It's over," I said.

Maggie, Jen, and Carla, with the help of Travis and Ray, got the horses groomed and saddled in record time. When Ms. Mansfield drove up, they had all four horses ready and waiting.

Tommy and Eric jumped out of the van. I waited to see David, but Ms. Mansfield got out and closed the doors, and still no David Miller appeared. Eric ran to his protest spot in the center of the arena and plopped down.

"Where's David?" Carla asked Ms. Mansfield, as she came out of the barn. Bruiser sidestepped, restless under the big show saddle.

"David's mother phoned and said she'd drive him here herself," Ms. Mansfield said. When she noticed my crutches, she acted genuinely concerned. I was glad to be able to tell her it had nothing to do with the horses. We took our seats and watched.

It wasn't easy to sit and leave the lesson to my friends. Maggie spent too much time on tricks, and Jen talked way too long about the culture of the Old West. But it didn't seem to matter. The two riders, Tommy and B.C., had never ridden better. And I got to look at things from a different angle.

Eric refused to ride Red, but he was content to sit a few feet away from the horse. A couple of times, when he didn't think anyone was watching, I caught Eric reaching over and petting the Chestnut.

David never did show up, so Carla talked Travis into riding Bruiser. From my ringside seat, I had a chance to observe the Pinto closely. I noticed that Bruiser acted fine until something weighed on his back. When Travis rode him a little too close to us, Ms. Mansfield scurried out of her chair. But I caught sight of something I hadn't noticed before. The oversized saddle wasn't sitting squarely on Bruiser's back. He looked uncomfortable.

While the boys listened to Maggie, Carla and I talked about Bruiser. Together, we came up with the idea that what he needed was a different saddle. "That would explain why he did so well when you rode him English," I told Carla.

"And when you rode him bareback," Carla said. "David won't like losing his fancy show saddle for tomorrow's performance." She stared down the lane. "I wonder where he is."

We got Travis to unsaddle Bruiser and try one of our lighter saddles on him. For the first 10 minutes, it didn't seem to make any difference. But then it was as if Bruiser realized the show saddle was gone. He relaxed and stopped sidestepping.

Travis rode Bruiser up to me, which made Ms. Mansfield drag her chair inside the barn. "Can you believe how well he's riding?" Travis asked. He reached up and stroked Bruiser under his mane. The horse stood perfectly still. "You think it was the saddle all along? Could that really be what made him act up before?"

"Pain makes horses do crazy things," I said. "They can't tell us about it in words. So they act out their pain. I can't believe I didn't see it before now."

At the end of the lesson, Jen walked over to Eric, took his hand, and led him and Red over to me. "I was just telling Eric here about my fear repellant."

"Is she making it up?" Eric asked.

I had never heard of anything like a fear repellant, but I'd prayed God would help me trust, to join up with my friends and work as a team. "I'll tell you the truth, Eric," I said. "I haven't heard of fear repellant before. But I trust Jen. And if she says she knows of one, I'd say you can trust her."

Jen grinned at me. "Here's how it works, Eric."

Here we go again—one of Jen's long, drawn-out explanations that will put Eric to sleep. But I didn't stop her. Instead, I prayed. I prayed that Jen would say the things Eric needed to hear.

Jen sat on the ground by my feet, and Eric sat beside her. "Red is a great horse," she began, "but he gets scared. And if *you're* scared, he gets even more scared. Horses can smell fear."

"I can't help getting scared," Eric whined.

"I know, Eric," Jen said. "About a hundred years ago, men who worked with wild stallions used to be scared of them. They couldn't help it either. But they discovered something they called *horse oils*. People couldn't smell the oils. But when the horse handlers rubbed it on their hands and foreheads, the stallions were fascinated by the scent and stayed calm."

"Do you have the horse oils?" Eric asked.

"I do," Jen answered. "I make my own. It just covers up the adrenaline smell that horses pick up on when we're afraid. Red will think you're the bravest rider in the world."

"I'll do it!" Eric said. "My mom and dad are coming tomorrow to watch me in the show. Do you think I can still ride Red?"

"I'm sure of it," Jen said.

Eric ran over to Red and stroked his mane.

"Nice going, Jen," I said.

"Look at Maggie," Jen whispered. "I've never seen her this patient. Tommy either, for that matter."

Maggie was teaching Tommy how to get the giant Blue Roan to bow. And little by little, Dusty was learning. When Dusty's neck arched low enough to be considered a bow, Maggie had Tommy toss his cowboy hat high in the air. With Carla's help, B.C. and Babe followed suit, bowing. Then B.C. tossed his hat in the air just like Tommy had done, as if the boys were partners.

It was amazing. Toes, fingers, shoulders, head, we were working together as one body. It felt right.

Ms. Mansfield had stayed in the shade of the barn. She stood up suddenly and gazed out toward the lane where a big, green car was driving up. "I think that's David now," she said. "He's missed the whole lesson." She walked across the paddock and waved to them.

Carla was at that end of the paddock. She watched as Ms. Mansfield motioned for the driver to come and join us. A thin woman who must have been David's mother got out of the car. I couldn't see anybody else inside though. She met Ms. Mansfield at the fence, and the two women seemed deep in conversation.

Maggie and Jen called in Dusty and Babe and started cooling the horses. Travis did the same with Bruiser. Carla was still standing at the far end of the paddock, a few yards from Ms. Mansfield and Mrs. Miller, who were still talking.

I started to holler for Carla to bring in Red and cool him down, but I stopped myself just in time. Maybe there was a reason Carla was staying out in the paddock. The longer I watched, the more convinced I became that she was lip-reading, keeping her eye on the conversation between Ms. Mansfield and David's mother.

B.C. ran up to me, his face flushed with excitement. "Did you see me? Did you see how I rode Babe? And how Tommy and I threw our hats way up in the air? Eric says he's going to do it too! I think we did better because David wasn't there to be mean to us. Maybe he won't come tomorrow. Do you think he'll come tomorrow? I really, really hope he won't come tomorrow!"

I was only half-listening to my brother. Carla had my attention. She was leading Red toward us, and she looked sad.

When she got close enough, I asked her, "What's wrong, Carla?"

She glanced toward Ms. Mansfield. The green car was driving off, and Ms. Mansfield was shouting for Eric and Tommy to get in the van.

"I probably shouldn't say anything," Carla said, sucking on her bottom lip.

"What, Carla? You have to say," I insisted. "We're a team now. If something's upsetting you, we want to know about it."

"Know about what?" Maggie asked. She and Jen walked out of the barn and joined us.

Carla seemed to think it over. Then she sighed. "That was Mrs. Miller, David's mother."

"I figured," Maggie said.

"I ... I know it's wrong, but I eavesdropped on them. I read her lips when she was talking to Ms. Mansfield."

"And ... ?" I said, wanting to hurry her up.

"And ... and I know why David wasn't here today," she said. She looked at me. "Did you know David has leukemia?"

"Leukemia?" I felt stunned. All that came to my mind were pictures of sick kids in hospital wards. How could he have leukemia and ride a horse? How could he have leukemia and be such a bully?

"What's ... what's luke-mah?" B.C. asked.

"It's a kind of cancer in your blood, B.C.," Jen said.

"Does it hurt him?" B.C. asked.

Does it hurt him? Was David in pain the same way Bruiser was? Bruiser's pain had made him act like a bully. Maybe David's pain had made him do the same thing.

"I don't know, B.C.," I said. "It probably hurts him." I turned to Carla. "But he couldn't have just gotten leukemia, right? I mean, he must have been doing okay with it. What happened? Did he get worse?"

"I don't think that's it," Carla said. "I missed some of what Mrs. Miller said when Ms. Mansfield stepped in the way. But from what I could understand, David is well enough to ride horses. That's not the problem."

"So what *is* the problem?" Maggie asked.

"His mother said David had chemotherapy treatments," Carla said.

Before B.C. could ask, Jen explained. "Chemotherapy is like a really strong medicine, B.C. It kills cells and stops the disease from spreading."

"And it makes people lose their hair," Carla said. "From what I could lip-read, that's the real problem."

"I don't understand," Jen said.

"David's hair has been falling out fast. That's why he's been taking his cowboy hat home and showing up in it for every practice. That's why he won't take off the hat." Carla paused and glanced at the center of the arena. "And that's why he didn't come to practice, why he's not coming to the show tomorrow. He doesn't want to throw his hat in the air and have everybody see how bald he is."

"That's terrible!" Maggie said. "It's all my fault. Me and my stupid Wild West Show! Why did I make such a big deal about tossing our hats in the air?"

"You didn't know, Maggie," I said. "It's not your fault." I pictured skinny David running his fingers through his thick, black hair, the one feature he seemed to be proud of.

"Is there anything we can do?" Jen asked. "I feel so awful for him."

"Me too," Carla said. "He drove me nuts

when he rode Bruiser. I wish I'd been nicer to him."

"You were great with David, Carla," I said, remembering how she'd always at least acted glad to see him. "He really likes you. He was hard to handle, like Bruiser." A bully like Bruiser, I thought, thinking about the show saddle hurting Bruiser's back and making him act up. Two bullies in pain.

We were all quiet for a minute. Suddenly, B.C. took off running.

"B.C.!" I shouted.

He didn't turn around or slow down.

Travis and Ray came out of the barn. I'd forgotten about them. "Want me to go after B.C.?" Travis asked.

"No," I answered. "He'll be all right. You can give me a lift home though, if you don't mind."

Travis looked shocked. "Are you actually asking me for a ride? For help?"

I tried to smile back at Travis. But the weight of what we'd learned about David Miller pressed in on me. I wondered how things might have been different if Carla, Maggie, Jen, and I had joined up earlier and put our heads together to help David. I said a prayer that God would give us another opportunity.

18

Saturday clouds spotted the blue sky with the first tease of rain we'd had in weeks. By the time Dotty had dropped me off at Horsefeathers, my friends had taken care of everything. Bruiser wore the lighter saddle. Horses were fed and groomed, stalls cleaned and mucked.

"What's up with your brother and my brother?" Jen asked, taking my crutches so I could sit on a bale of hay. Dogless Cat bounded up from nowhere and settled onto my lap.

"I have no idea about Tommy," I said. "But B.C. sure was acting mysterious. He and Dotty left the house an hour ago. Dotty came back without him and wouldn't tell me where he was."

"He was with Tommy," Travis said, checking the girth on Bruiser's saddle. "Dotty and B.C. drove by and picked him up. Mom wouldn't tell us where they went. But Dotty promised to have them here on time for the show."

"What about David?" I asked. "Have you talked to Ms. Mansfield, Travis? Did she tell you if David's coming or not?"

"All she said was that she didn't need me to drive. Parents will drive their kids in."

Horsefeathers filled up fast. Mr. and Mrs. Zucker staked out a whole section of the arena and lined up their kids along the fence. Mrs. Zucker would have been a trusty Welsh Cob if she'd been a horse. She carried one of the triplets in a back-pack carrier, and held the other two in her arms. Mr. Zucker had his hands full trying to keep track of the twins and Rebecca.

Eric's parents came, but Eric wasn't with them. I got Maggie to make the rounds with me and introduce ourselves and Horsefeathers to parents and board members. I let Maggie do the talking and charm our spectators, while I kept an anxious eye out for our King's Kamp riders. With five minutes to go, the boys still hadn't shown up.

Carla ran up to us just as Maggie was complimenting one of the board member's shoes. "Scoop!" Carla shouted. "Dotty's here. Looks like she's got a car-full."

The Chevy's doors opened, and out came all four of our King's Kamp riders, dressed in jeans and T-shirts, their cowboy hats already on. I wondered how Dotty ... or B.C. ... had gotten David to come. But I shot up a quick prayer of thanks that he had.

The boys ran to the fence and climbed over. David reached the top first. But instead of pushing Tommy off or calling Eric and B.C. names, he stopped at the top and gave Eric a hand up. Carla saw it too. We exchanged smiles, and I felt a chill travel down my spine.

I was getting along better and using only one crutch. I held Red and Babe while Jen took Eric into the hayloft and let him dab on the fear potion. When he came out, he didn't hesitate. He walked straight to Red, stuck his foot in the stirrup and mounted. Red stood perfectly still.

Tommy Zucker shouted, "Way to go, Eric!" Then Maggie helped him climb up on Dusty.

B.C. mounted Babe by himself. In the audience, I spotted Ms. Mansfield. She stood in the center of the group of board members. I hoped she'd only pass on the good stuff about Horse-feathers and our King's Kamp lessons.

David ran to Bruiser. "Hey! Where's my saddle?" he asked Carla.

"This is your saddle today," Carla said.

"I want the show saddle!" David yelled.

The audience got quiet and focused on the David drama unfolding. I saw David's parents start to come in after their son. The whole show could go down the drain in an instant if David threw a fit.

B.C. and Babe stood a few feet from Bruiser and David. "David," B.C. said, "that other saddle hurt Bruiser. That's why he acted funny. He was in pain."

David swung around and stared at the Pinto. "I don't want you to hurt," he said softly. "I didn't know." Then he stuck his foot in the stirrup and mounted.

The show went better than any of us could have hoped for. The boys followed Maggie and Moby in a figure 8. The audience clapped through the whole thing. Ms. Mansfield looked as proud as if she'd invented the horses herself.

Before the finale of the show, Travis ran up to me. "Scoop," he said, "Ms. Mansfield just told me the board's already made their decision."

I stared into his deep blue eyes and got my answer before he told me.

"King's Kamp is taking the horses," he said.

I hugged Travis, then turned to my partners, Jen and Maggie and Carla, and whispered the good news to them one by one.

"Bring in your horses!" Maggie called to the riders. She lowered her voice for the boys, "We'll make the horses bow, and then that will be that."

"But what about tossing our hats?" Tommy asked.

"We aren't going to do that," Maggie said. She fidgeted with one of her braids that stuck out from her cowboy hat.

"But you said all Wild West Shows end with the cowboys tossing their hats," Eric said.

"But that doesn't mean ... I mean, we don't have to ..." Maggie said.

I could tell how nervous Maggie was, afraid she'd say the wrong thing and make things worse for David.

Maggie made her horse rear. "And now, ladies and gentlemen," she shouted, "King's Kamp would like to thank you for coming to our show and being such a great audience!"

Slowly and with a couple of false starts, the horses took their bows.

"Now!" B.C. shouted. "Toss your hats on the count of *three!*"

"No, B.C.!" I cried.

He ignored me, and so did Eric and Tommy. I saw their hands go to their hats. David looked worried. He glanced from one to the other, frowning. His hand slammed down on his own hat.

"Don't!" Maggie pleaded.

"One!" B.C. shouted. "Two! Three!"

Three hats came off and sailed through the air. My gaze went from the hats to my brother's head—my brother's *bald* head. And his wasn't the only bald head. Eric and Tommy had shaved their heads too. They grinned sheepishly under heads bald as eggs.

David Miller stared in wide-eyed amazement. Tears trailed from the corners of his eyes. He grabbed his hat and flung it into the crowd, so far I lost sight of it and imagined it was flying all the way to heaven, a gift for Jesus.

The whole arena fell silent. Then a crack of thunder split the silence, followed by a deafening rumble. I looked up and saw dark clouds moving in fast, closing out the sunlight that had reflected off four bald heads. And just like that, the sky split open and rain fell in torrents.

The crowd burst into laughter, as grateful as the parched earth for the miraculous rain. Nobody ran for cover from the fat drops of water. Faces turned skyward, and arms stretched out to embrace the rain. In the center of the arena, horses whinnied, cooled by the showers. And water splatted and bounced off B.C., Tommy, Eric, and David.

Dotty had come up behind me as I watched the miracles unfold. "It was all B.C.'s idea," she said. "He called them boys hisself. Their mamas give me the okay to take them up to the barber shop this morning and get their heads shaved. B.C. said he didn't want David to feel like he was all alone." She put a hand on my shoulder. "I don't reckon I've ever been more proud of that boy."

I put my hand on Dotty's. "I don't know if you're a toe or a heart, Dotty," I said, "but I'm awful glad we're part of the same body."

We stayed there as water soaked the ground and bathed the horses, and rain caressed four bald heads, the King's kids who had joined up for a miracle none of us would ever get over.

Horse Signals

Observe a horse, and you can pick up on signals that may let you know how the horse is feeling.

Ears

Loosely forward ears — All is well. The horse is just listening and attending to sounds around him or her.

Uneven ears — (one up, one back; swiveling) The horse is relaxed and merely paying attention.

Pricked forward ears — The horse is startled, or on the alert to something up ahead.

Stiff, flicking, or twitching ears — Heads up! The horse may be close to terror and ready to bolt.

Flat back, pinned-down ears — Be careful! The horse is angry. He or she may be thinking about biting or kicking.

Airplane ears — (ears lopped to the sides) The horse is tired or bored.

Droopy ears — The horse is either sleepy, or in pain.

Tail

Clamped down tail — The horse is frightened.

High tail — (tail held high) The horse is excited, feeling his oats, and thinking about how fun it would be to "hightail" it out of there.

Tail swishes in circles — The horse is very anxious or unhappy.

Tail switches constantly — It's probably fly season!

Horse Talk

Much of "horse talk" remains a mystery. Sounds vary in pitch, duration, loudness and can have various meanings according to the circumstances. Here are some explanations of the sounds horses make, and some general ideas of what might be on a horse's mind when he or she speaks:

Nicker — A soft, partially nasal sound, usually fairly short. Nickers can be greeting from one horse to another or from a horse to a human friend. Some horses nicker in anticipation of getting their oats or just to let others know they're around.

Neigh — An open-mouthed sound, louder than the nicker. It's the next step up from a nicker and can be heard from farther away. Mares might neigh to call their foals. Other horses may neigh to announce that the barn has come into view, or to call other horses to attention.

Whinny — A high-pitched sound, louder than the nicker or the neigh. When horses whinny, they are usually excited about something.

Bellow — A deep sound, louder than the whinny. Generally, horses are either angry or declaring their rightful authority, as a stallion claiming a herd or threatening an invader.

Squeal — A throaty burst of high-pitched sound. Mares and foals can exchange squeals in play or in earnest. It may be a burst of excitement or enthusiasm, as a horse ready to give a playful buck.

Scream — A loud, high cry that sounds like a scream. It usually indicates an emergency—fear, pain, rage.

Snort — A blowing out from the nostrils. Horses snort out of impatience or playfulness.

Sigh — Horses make other sounds, such as a chesty sigh. It may mean they're content or ready for a nap.

Groan — A steady, throaty sound. Some horses groan from discomfort; others groan out of habit, as groaning on a long trail ride.

Photo by Brad Ruebensaal

About the Author

Dandi Daley Mackall rode her first horse—
bareback—when she was 3. She's been riding ever
since. She claims some of her best friends have
been horses she and her family have owned:
mixed-breeds, quarter horses, American Saddle
Horses, Appaloosas, Pintos, and Paints.

When she isn't riding, Dandi is writing. She has
published more than 200 books for children and
adults, including *The Cinnamon Lake Mysteries*
and *The Puzzle Club Mysteries,* both for Concordia. Dandi has written for *Western Horseman* and
other magazines as well. She lives in rural Ohio,
where she rides the trails with her husband Joe
(also a writer), children Jen, Katy, and Dan, and
the real Moby and Cheyenne.